TWELVE SCORCHING DAYS

Also by Melanie Greene

Pier 3 Coffee Series

Mocha for Mateo *(Alicia & Mateo)*

Cappuccino for Callie *(Abraham & Callie)*

Latte for Leyla *(Austin & Leyla)*

Roll of the Dice Series

Rocket Man *(Serena & Dillon)*

Ready to Roll *(Janice & Miguel)*

Eye of the Tiger *(Natalie & Evan)*

Let the Good Times Roll *(Chloe & Gabriel)*

Roll of a Lifetime *(Rachel & Theo)*

Roll Play *(Kim-ly & Tómas)*

On a Roll *(Gillian & Vic)*

Roll in the Hay *(Anton & Cisco) - available to subscribers or as a bonus in the Roll of the Dice novella anthology*

Other Contemporary Romances

Retreat to Love *(Ashlyn & Caleb)*

Feather in Her Cap *(Jeannie & Brendan)*

Twelve Scorching Days *(Sarita & Scorch)*

Margo of the Bells (Margo & Karl)

Curiosity (Amity & Josh) - story in the It's Always Been You anthology

TWELVE SCORCHING DAYS

MELANIE GREENE

First print edition: October 2022

Twelve Scorching Days/by Melanie Greene

Cover Design by Melanie Greene

ISBN: 978-1-941967-42-3

CHAPTER

ONE

SCORCH

Stroke of midday, and the warm December breeze wafted me up from the shore to the door of my rental cottage. I dropped my sand-coated shoes next to my duffle and propped the guitar case against the porch rail while I scrolled through my phone for the arrival instructions.

I had to turn it off airplane mode, which meant a barrage of notifications. The first I'd read since crossing the New Mexico border. My band—my ex-band—The Evil Stepbrothers had only just finished up our latest tour. Everything I thought could stay backstage until we got off the road, instead blew up there, as public as possible. The headline writers were having a ball, as every one of my notifications made clear.

The Evil Stepbrothers Burn Scorch On Stage

After Phoenix Flameout, Can Scorch Madigan's Career Rise from the Ashes?

'No Prince Charming': TES's Haddon and Lewis on Madigan's Bitter Backstage Brawling

Brawling, for fucks sake. It had never been a brawl, but

truth had no weight against the lure of alliteration. And with two against me, and those two eager to spread all kinds of toxicity about me, I moved fast. I arranged with my pal Brendan to stay at his in-laws' beach place for a couple of weeks, threw some stuff in a rental car, turned off my phone, hit I-10, and drove the thousand miles to this little Gulf Coast cottage.

I loved a long drive. I loved the hours to stare at scenery and let my thoughts churn. I loved the solitude, the detours, the random roadside diners. Watching the shadows crawl across the day, and spotting a nondescript place to hold up for the night.

Being away from the band I'd been sucked into at nineteen and found near impossible to escape. Until that humiliating set at the indie festival propelled me away from them and into an unknown future. My life was an hourglass draining me of all my cultural relevance, and I had to get it flipped before I had no career left at all.

The place was all grey-weathered wood and candy-hued trim. Cozy, and just obtrusive enough for me to spy it waiting for me while I counteracted the long drive with a wander through the surrounding sand dunes. Gave me a feeling of possibility. Of hope. Settled down my jitters about all I needed to accomplish during this creative retreat. The too-bright pressure of the world's expectations for me. Of my expectations for myself. I just had to figure out how to get in and start to get my life in order. Muting the notifications, I found Brendan's message. Parking rules, advice about the veranda's tricksy solar shade, door code.

I stepped in, and saw great beauty, and felt great pain.

Gasping, the beauty dropped her broom and dustpan and dashed to wrap her arms around me. Before I was aware of my own curses, she had me deposited in an armchair and was kneeling with my foot on her lap.

"Oh, ouch!"

Somewhere under my disbelief, I registered the lilting alto of her voice. I pushed a long breath through clenched teeth. "Are you really the one saying 'ouch' right now?"

The smooth look she arched my way contradicted her quick, efficient handling of my goddamn throbbing foot. "Excuse my sympathy. It was just a reflex from working with children. They tend to calm down if you let them know they're not alone with their pain."

Unbelievable. "I'm not sure how often you leave shards of glass laying around for your students to step in, but it may be a good idea to come up with another way to bond with them."

Ignoring me, she pulled a green kerchief off her head, slapped it on the edge of a coffee table, and yanked the table forward so she could rest my bloody foot on it. "Don't move. I'm going to grab some supplies."

And then she was down the hall. Well, not hall. The cottage wasn't really big enough for a hall. I focused on the sounds of banging around and water running until she returned. "I can't find tweezers, but I think I can get most of the pieces out without them. After I do that, I'll wrap it up and drive you to urgent care. I'm Sarita, by the way."

"Ignatius." Never had the syllables of my real name grated more painfully as I forced them out. I took perverse satisfaction in the way she winced.

"Right, Brendan said. Jeannie's my sister."

I saw it now. Same wave of dark hair, same strong chin. And no offense to my friends, but Brendan's wife paled in comparison to her sister. If she hadn't been the one who caused my agony, I'd cast her as my ministering angel.

If angels swore under their breaths as they prodded at my ripped up flesh. I fought against thinking about the extent of the damage, but her furrowed brow wasn't helping. And it had been a lot of glass, the shards now exploded across the floor around us. "Hi, Jeannie's sister. You're not sitting on glass yourself, are you?"

She glanced around and shook her head before bending back to blot up more of my blood. I closed my eyes and tilted my head back against the chair. Urgent care. Splintered glass. Sandy feet. I wanted to scream. Or cry. Or call my mom. Or otherwise bash myself against the cage of performative masculinity and let my vulnerable side freak the fuck out.

"Shit. Okay. This hurts like hell, and I'm going to just sit here and breathe deep for a minute, if you don't mind. Can you talk? Are you a rambler? I'm longing for some chatter right about now to distract me."

She huffed a laugh. "Never been accused of rambling before, but, yes, sure, I'll give it a go. I mean, I said sorry, right? I think I did. I shouldn't even have been the one cleaning the place, you know? My plan was, come to town just for the party, but no. My godmother and her family decided to stay with us, so I get the royal decree: show up for all of my holiday break. And then you're coming, and the cleaning service is double booked for the season, so hey, why not send Sarita down to tidy the cottage and put out some Christmas decorations?"

"I hate Christmas decorations."

Her hands stilled for a minute. "Well. That's weird."

I grunted. Not the first thing about me someone called weird.

"You'll be so glad I broke the ornament ball, then. Except for the part where I couldn't find an empty box to sweep the shards into, and you stomped all over the damn thing."

"Except for that."

Her palm wrapped across the top of my ankle and squeezed. Warm and gentle and almost enough to short out the pain transmitters racing up and down my leg. "Okay. Sit there a minute so I can sweep again. You have shoes somewhere?"

I waved back towards the porch. "With my gear. Don't think I can put them on, though."

"Just the one. No need to extend the damage to the left foot, too."

"Right. You mind bringing in my guitar, too?" I eased forward to examine the layers of gauze on my foot. Already blood dotted the outer layers.

Welcome to vacation, Scorch. Supposed to bleed all over the page, not the floor.

Sarita returned with a damp towel and my shoe. I blotted my face and hands—sweatier in the aftermath of the injury than when I was walking in the sun—then cleaned away sand so I could stand.

She winced as she helped balance me. "You want a pain killer or something? It's about twenty minutes to the clinic."

"Shit. Um. Yeah, thanks. And a glass of water."

She was a blur of energy as I stood there, foot throbbing, eyeing the distance to the door. When she rolled a desk chair in from the bedroom I didn't try to hide my relief.

"Your chariot, sir."

Wasn't sure how I felt about her making jokes at my expense, what with her being the one to blame in the first place, but that didn't stop me from leaning on her strong shoulder as I hopped out to where she'd set the chair on the walkway. With my knee resting on the chair, we wheeled me towards the fancy car beside mine at the curb.

"I'm gonna get blood all over your upholstery."

"Okay."

Okay then. Not my problem. Sarita drove like a native Texan, which is to say, like everyone should stay the hell out of her way. Irritated in general as I was with her, I admired her back-off-or-I'll-make-you-sorry attitude. I would be adopting the same, soon as possible. Soon as I got over the damn painful and aggravating disruption she'd shoved in my way. Only so many times I'd hand someone the chance to ruin every step I needed to take. I vowed this setback from Sarita would be the last disruption to my plan.

Triage had me on a table right away, hooked up to a few monitors, handing over insurance info and answering intake questions.

The whole time, Sarita stood there. Hovering. Interjecting. Ignoring the constant blip of her phone notifications.

"You need to get that?" I finally asked.

She went blank.

"Your phone's blowing up."

Her hand darted to the ass pocket of her denim shorts. "Crap. Sorry."

"Whatever. Look, I'll get a car when I'm done here."

Her frown stayed directed at her screen. "What?"

"This town has Lyft? Taxis? I'll call for a ride when I'm done. You can go."

Maybe I was surly but she didn't have to gape at me. "I'm not going to just leave you alone."

"I'm not alone." I waved towards the bustling in the

hallway. "There are trained medical people here. I don't need you now."

Another three chimes from her phone, and I was ready to throw the thing through the window. Safer target than the beeping of my blood pressure and oxygen and whatever else monitors. Have I mentioned I'm on-edge about medical stuff? No story of early trauma or anything; all I can think to blame it on is this one babysitter who played nonstop *ER* reruns.

So the last thing I needed was another machine demanding attention in the room, even if it wanted Sartia's attention instead of mine. She was studying me like I had inscrutable lyrics scrolling up my face, and I went and pulled a dick move. Lip curl and everything. "Like what you see, sweetie? You hanging around so you can apologize in a more physical way?"

Even that didn't deter her. "Have you already picked up groceries?"

Record scratch. I dropped the lewd act. "What?"

"For your stay. There's fresh milk and some eggs and bread, but not much else. Did you stop at the store on your way in?"

Ah. I glanced at my foot. I wouldn't be driving anytime soon. "I'll find someone to deliver."

She lifted that stubborn chin and rolled her eyes. "Okay, what are your faves? Allergies, comfort foods? I'll go get stuff while you're getting patched up."

Before I could skewer the plan and assure her I knew how to use DoorDash, she took a call. And since she didn't leave the confines of my exam room, I didn't bother pretending I wasn't listening. Some family member, voice emphatic even filtered through the electronics, telling her to come home and do something social. Sarita saying I needed her around. Saying I wouldn't be okay with someone taking her place. Saying it must be the temperamental rock star in me, and that Jeannie and Brendan would be irked if she pissed me off.

Ha. I had five angry texts half-composed in my head. Only hadn't sent because I didn't want to deal with Brendan's fussing.

Medical people came in with a distracting tray of shiny implements. They got busy digging into my sole, so I got busy analyzing every word Sarita said. She claimed someone named Luis would be fine without her. She dispatched a sister to sweep up all the bloody glass in my temporary living room. She swore Luis would text her if he needed any old friend's number.

Fuck but everything the doctor was doing hurt.

Sarita turned and saw, I presume, a sheen of flop sweat on my face. "Gotta go. Scorch needs me."

I'd have denied it, but she squeezed my hand without asking, and hell if I didn't squeeze back.

Everything was collapsing around me. My limbs still felt coated in that mix of cleaning products and dirt that adhered to me whenever I got near the vicinity of a duster. I was getting thirty-six texts a minute from my relatives. Lies about the whole situation were rolling off my tongue like a not-broken Christmas ornament skittering across the floor.

Oh, and I totally was to blame for who knows what kind of damage to the super hot rock god who was gripping my hand like I could haul him out of his miserable, scandal-ridden life and set him on a path to comfort and ease.

Scorch—or Ignatius, maybe he meant me to call him—glared at my phone. And at my face. And at the motivational poster plastered to the ceiling above him. It was a fine glare: very angry, very clear about his mood. Except it slipped every time the doctor sucked his teeth or reached for a different set of tiny tweezers. Then his face blanched, and his hold on me tightened, and I got real familiar with how dark his muddy eyes looked when his pupils were dilated in fear.

Don't ask me what I'd been thinking, to leave the pile of broken glass so close to the door. The blasted ball slipped out of my hands and shattered and the broom was leaning against the kitchen counter so I started there and swept everything towards the nearest open space. Not thinking Scorch would walk in, barefoot or not, until I'd taken myself and all my mess out of the place.

He hissed when the doctor wriggled his toes, searching for any more debris to clean out.

"So what do you want for lunch? Are you into tacos?"

He rolled his eyes, but kept my hand. "Obviously. Who's not into tacos?"

"Okay. Good answer. I'll go buy your Cheerios and steak or what have you, and pick up some tacos from the truck next to the market. Their carne guisado will make you forget all your pain. Hopefully you'll be all patched up by then and I can take you home."

Half a smile! What a vast change from the Glare of Death. "Fine. Give me your number, I'll forward my shopping list. Does the cottage have a blender?"

I nodded, and did not giggle. Scorch Madigan kept a grocery list on his phone. That was going in the sibling group text as soon as I left the room.

Details settled, I left him trying to figure out if he was due for a tetanus shot and scooted to my car. Ridiculous to savor four minutes of solitude as I drove to the HEB, but it had been a hectic month—the usual winter concert rush, heading to the coast for the holiday break—and there was no hint I'd be left alone until January. Not with my godmother and her family filling the house, and everything that entailed.

So, yeah. Four minutes of alone time in my car. Just me and my headphones as I navigated the store aisles. Leaning against my bumper, devouring a boat of flamin hot nachos while I waited for our tacos. The next two weeks was all about savoring my every solitary second.

Okay, and maybe doing a few things to help out Scorch while I was at it. Only because of the injury, not because I'd spent any time following his career and the whole previous day checking the internet for analyses of the #BattleOfThe-Band, as the most trending hashtag labeled it.

Thing is, once your sister starts showing up regularly on the Grammys red carpet, and dropping the names of her husband's music industry friends, you just can't help picking up a few bits of interest in some of them. Especially the ones who make you thirsty as a boat of flamin hot nachos.

Scorch hovered on his crutches when I pulled back up. We got him and his well-encased foot settled in the car and I handed over his tacos. His groan of appreciation was the first friendly sound he'd made since we met. Not that I blamed him. But I definitely liked the way his eyes crinkled as he made short work of his lunch.

Damn but he was fit and fine. Too bad he kinda hated me.

Once we got back to the cottage, he was Mr. Stubborn about navigating himself inside, but at least he didn't pull any macho nonsense about me bringing in his groceries. Between trips to the car, I grabbed a stack of thick paperbacks from the shelf of beach reads by the TV and built up a little pedestal on the coffee table. I topped it with a cushion and nudged Scorch into propping up his foot. He pretty much sat there in a daze while I arranged the kitchen and took his duffle into the bedroom. Too intimate to unpack it for him? Whatever. We'd gone down a road together and if he cared that I saw his brightly patterned boxer-briefs, he would just have to get over it. My actions saved him from excessive standing, which was literally what the doctor ordered.

Still, I probably blushed a little when I returned to the living room. It was the dancing banana briefs. My brain blasted me with a best guess of how he'd look in them, and it was quite the picture. I cleared my throat. "Can I get you anything?"

He dragged open his eyes. "Oh. Yeah. Is there an ice pack or something? And is the beer cold?"

I'd stuck a couple bottles in the freezer, so one stop had all he needed. He wrapped the ice over his ankle and rested the beer on his forehead, shifting his eyes my way once I took the armchair beside him.

"Help yourself."

I shrugged. "So far, I'm the one who paid for it."

It took a good six seconds for him to turn his head from me, to his foot, and back to me. Scorch Madigan had stage presence, that was for sure. Swagger, timing, and a face he could make say it all.

I hadn't spent three-quarters of my life as a performer to back down, though. I swigged my beer.

"You can go now." So clipped. I could see it killed him that he broke the silence. He could see me see it. More scowling.

"You need my help."

"Beg pardon?"

"Discharge paperwork said to stay off it as much as possible. Way I read that is, help with food, getting stuff done, chores." My voice shuddered a little on that last word, but I covered it with another swallow. I'd told the family someone else should clean the place. They knew how much

I hated it. They'd palmed it on me anyway. Well, now I had an excuse to stay away from Luis, so it served them right.

"No need."

A future filled with Luis encounters stretched tediously ahead of me. "I'm offering."

"I'm refusing."

"How are you gonna stop me?" I waggled my set of cottage keys at him. "When I come back, want me to bring a guitar stand?"

He had his instrument balanced between the couch and coffee table, and it made me twitchy. It was a good piece, solid and well used. Faded over the frets, the leather strap shaped by Scorch's sweat, a glittering unicorn sticker below the saddle that somehow failed to look incongruous. He'd unloaded a messy pile of notebooks and paper alongside it, and stashed a pencil behind his ear. The man wanted me out of his way. His vacation wasn't starting on a high note, and I wasn't helping.

It would niggle at me in other circumstances. Circumstances that didn't include the forty-seven texts about Luis and Maxima and if I'd be back before lunch? Before they started baking? Before dinner, at least?

My phone dinged again. Make that forty-eight texts.

He leaned forward and snagged the longneck out of my hand. "Fine. If you have a spare stand, I'll take it. Tomorrow. Today, just pack up all this Christmas shit and clear out, yeah?"

He drained the rest of my beer, stacked the empty next to his, closed his eyes, and ignored me until I was gone.

CHAPTER

THREE

SCORCH

No idea what time it was. I woke and the place was bright. Yanking up the blankets to cover my head made me yelp from bedding dragging against my foot. So, recovery was going well. And my phone wouldn't stop ringing.

"What."

Pam Chang, the PR expert assigned to me by my manager, didn't even demand an apology for my rudeness before launching into work mode.

"Pam. Hold up." I scooped together some pillows to lean against as I hauled myself to sitting. The curtains were shoved back like I wanted to get an eyeful of wild sea oats and sand dunes first thing in the morning. "Are you saying word about my trip to urgent care already got out?"

"You were at urgent care? What the hell happened? Are you okay?"

She sounded like she cared for real, and not just so she could figure out how to spin it.

"Yeah. I mean, not yet, but it's fine. Cut up my foot pretty bad. If that's not what's out, what's happening?"

And that was all the permission she needed to tear into me. What was I doing so far away? Why Texas? Who was I with? What about the interviews she'd set up? And most vital of all, was I really suing TES for music rights?

"Yes."

Pam paused at last. Held her silence.

"I'm going solo, Pam. They want to claim some stuff they rejected after two chords, never even got close to performing."

"You can't do that."

I sighed real loud down the line. She hated that. "Yeah. I can, actually." I'd talked with everyone. My mom, my manager and lawyer, and when I knew my game plan, with the band.

"But they're already crucifying your reputation. This is going to escalate in all kinds of bad ways. You know their narrative about you riding their coattails to fame."

I grunted something. Fact was, they'd been on their way up when I came along, and fine. Okay. Say whatever about fragile musician egos, but they'd been more than clear throughout our last tour. Haddon and Lewis 'weren't sure' anymore what I brought to the table. Some songwriting. A great voice and skillful guitar. The stubborn pride that kept me showing up on time, willing to do shit to make The Evil Stepbrothers shine. Nothing irreplaceable.

Like hell I agreed with them. All the insidious comments, all the brash put-downs, all the subtweeting. They pushed their narrative until I pushed back, and ended up trending for none of the right reasons. So they could blast their opinion about me all they wanted, now their bile was out in the open.

Fact was, I didn't *want* to bring myself to their table anymore.

I wanted a table of my own.

After promising eight times to review everything she'd forward to me, I hung up on Pam and sank into the bed. Couldn't have been three blessed minutes of silence later when I heard the jangle of keys. Too much to have hoped that she'd have lost the damn things, I suppose.

I debated my best move. Pretend to be asleep, or swagger around in my underwear? As if I could swagger on crutches. But if I could deliver a blow to the stick up her ass, maybe she would depart without me needing to yell at Jeannie's little sister. Jeannie's icy, hot little sister.

Yeah, the memory of her lifting the tail of her shirt to slide the phone from her back pocket was a factor. And the curve of her neck as she swallowed my beer. May as well have some fun while annoying the beauty into leaving, I figured.

Best laid plans. Getting myself out of the bathroom without crashing against the door was a trick I hadn't mastered. I showed up in the kitchen with a ridiculous sheen of sweat across my chest, like I was halfway through a stadium show. So much for giving Sarita as much attitude as she gave me.

But I hadn't been performing for a decade to back off in the face of one imperious stare. "Isn't there some kind of tradition around here of knocking before you enter some-one's place?"

She didn't drop the perfect poise, but her gaze was darting all up and down my body. *Ha.* I slid onto the stool beside where she was whisking up some eggs and dropped the crutches so I was cleared to cross my arms over my chest. Woman liked biceps, it seemed. Ha.

"I put the coffee on." Her voice was a tad scratchy, like

she'd fallen to a fast sleep after panting through some intense bed play, and woke up sated but dehydrated.

I snagged the pad of paper on the counter and jotted down 'sated / dehydrated.'

Could use a glass of something cool myself, but I wasn't going to navigate on crutches while Sarita watched, and no way was I giving her the satisfaction of asking for it.

She had a nasty habit of deflating all my snits. The second I decided I wasn't asking for a drink, she set a glass of orange juice and my antibiotics on the counter beside me. Next up: toast and jam and scrambled eggs with fresh chives cut into them. And an apple. Washed but whole, like the message was: *I'm making sure you get nutrients, but I'm not your personal chef, so don't go making any demands on me.*

Fine. I could deliver my own message. I crunched into the thing. Five hearty bites, and I deposited it on my crumb-filled plate. Sarita didn't even glance my way. She went past me into my bedroom and I leaned back enough to glimpse her opening the dresser drawer.

"I put your clothes in there," she said, gesturing over her shoulder as she returned with my favorite Henley. "Do you want to try and shower, or just wash the foot on its own?"

How was she more imperious the more she helped me out? I leaned into the dirtbag role she'd assigned me. "Just the foot. Got a clean bucket or anything?"

She shook that disapproving, elegant head at me. "The bucket and mop and broom are in that closet behind you, in case you find yourself interested in cleaning at any point. You probably want to keep as much sand as you can out of here. For your foot's sake."

I crossed my arms again, because I was no fool. My biceps

looked just about as good in the Henley as they did bare. Especially when I was still fighting off a bit of an infection fever fog. "So the bucket's no good for my foot, is what you're saying?"

She didn't answer. At least, not in words. She just went to the kitchen cabinet and pulled out a mixing bowl and started to fill it with water. I swiveled on my stool and decided I could make it to the couch without the crutches. My heel wasn't too cut up, so in theory I could balance on it and just about walk.

I almost got sucked into the trap of manly expectations again, but it hurt like blazing hell, and I'd heard of a study that people who cursed when hurt had higher pain tolerance. So, yeah. I yelped and swore, even after lowering myself to the couch.

"If you need me to pick up your crutches off the floor next time, just let me know."

I ignored her.

I tried, anyhow. Hard to ignore someone kneeling and taking your foot in hand, examining it for any warning signs, submerging it into water the perfect temperature and gently washing it clean. Then there was the way she propped it in her warm lap to gently dry it and administer cream and a slight massage that let at least part of my aching limb relax.

Even the part of me that had ached overnight for Sarita managed to relax and soak in her ministrations. Well, mostly that was because I'd been very busy informing my cock that it would not get hard no matter how close Sarita got or how thoroughly she tended to me.

I needed my guitar for coverage.

In a moment. Just then, I'd fallen into a stupor. Between the pain, the frustration of not getting the long shore walks I'd counted on for inspiring me to write my solo album, and the way each notification on my phone curled me more into myself, my brain was in a dead zone. Okay; fine. It was part self-pity and part stupor.

Either way. I deserved a break from all the reality around me. Eyes closed, I registered Sarita propping my heel on that stack of books again, and was thinking about opening an eye to thank her for her help, when a series of honking squeaks shook me to alertness. They overlapped, and merged into a trill, and honked again. I started at Sarita. "The hell is that?"

She rose and glanced at the ceiling. Made a moue. "Probably just the ghosts."

I was not hearing this woman correctly. "The ghosts?"

"The ghosts of the beach. They always try to lure shore birds here with their call, but even the seagulls know they're a bad bet. I expect they'll be here off and on for a few days. Didn't Brendan and Jeannie warn you?"

Texting them to ask for the truth would be ridiculous. I refused to believe the cottage was haunted, unless it was by the ghosts of Christmases Past that Sarita hadn't yet packed up to take away.

She tried to sell me on the beach ghost story for a bit longer, but when the honking started again I headed to the window.

"You can't see them from there."

"The ghosts?"

This time she smirked. "The whooping cranes. They overwinter here. There's a family that hangs out a few hundred yards to the southeast, but you'll hear them far more than you'll see them."

Next, she grabbed an Audubon-type pamphlet off the bookshelf and got all chatty about habitat conservation and the birds that were no longer quite on the brink of extinction. Which was great—I'm all for any and all reversals of the destruction of our planet—but the thing I kept noticing was the way Sarita's eyes shone when she was excited. The way she tossed the shimmering length of her dark hair over her shoulder when she pointed out the series of framed photos of 'their' family of whoopers. The dimple that popped when she admitted she and her siblings had played an epic UNO tournament to determine who got to name 'their' birds.

Forget beach ghosts. I had a feeling I was going to be haunted by the specter of an animated Sarita, and would spend more time than I should coaxing it out of hiding.

FOUR

SARITA

Tens of thousands of things I'd leap to do rather than decorate cookies. Up to and including giving surly Scorch a sponge bath. Not that the man seemed concerned with cleanliness, as if his mussed hair and morning stubble and even the gummy, residual lines from the surgical tape above his ankle made no difference to him.

I shoved the whooper pamphlet in his hands and asked if he needed anything else to read, anything fetched or fixed up for his comfort.

He pushed himself to standing, then shook his head all slow and sexy. "You've got to get over this idea that just because I'm a rock god, I can't take care of my basic needs."

"I'm coming back to make your dinner."

On stage, he pulled this move for the intense-feelings songs. I'd seen it over and over watching concert footage last night. And on earlier occasions. It was a kind of cock-wise lean, his right side from shoulder to hip jutting forth like it couldn't stand any distance between him and the next body, plus a quick tap over his heart with his left hand before it sank back to the guitar strings. No guitar on him now, so when he pulled the move, he tapped his heart four times while saying, "I will count the seconds while we're apart."

Sarcastic ass.

Mama's ringtone sounded, which was a sure-fire escalation of her attempts to haul me back to her kitchen. I didn't think I'd been gone long enough to justify it, but I wasn't going to dismiss her. I snatched up my stuff and answered her on my way out the door.

"Princess, where are you? Are you still asleep? We're waiting on you in the kitchen."

"No, Mama, I'm at the cottage. I had to come out and help Ignatius with his breakfast, remember?" She remembered. We both knew it. But pretending she didn't was her way of showing disapproval.

"Well, we're all waiting on you in the kitchen."

I bit my tongue, because that was my job. That, and, it seemed, being in the kitchen two minutes ago. "On my way."

By 'all,' Mama meant her and Uncle Bill and my godmother Maxima, for the most part. They were the traditional trio when it came time to make Christmas cookies. They roped in as many as my siblings as possible, plus Maxima's son Luis, my nemesis. Well, not quite nemesis. We used to get along great. Unlucky for me, that was when we were teenagers, and our collective families decided we made a cute couple.

Which then meant that we were destined, and hey, if we got married some day Uncle Bill and Maxima could merge their companies and make an empire, also destined to be ruled by my cutely-coupled self and Luis.

Yes, I'd pointed out that our families were more than

close enough already, and Bill's and Maxima's hospitality not-quite-empires were already in each other's pockets. They didn't need to force Luis and me into matrimony to merge, if that's what they wanted. Never mind that I had zero interest in running a company. Mama pretended my music degree was secretly in business management somehow. No use trying to convince her otherwise.

I don't know what made Uncle Bill switch from, "I hope your Luis marries one of my lovely nieces one day," to, "Luis and Sarita are going to make us so proud; I will cry every second of their wedding day."

Whatever it was, his fantasy spread throughout the rest of the generation we siblings called the 'elders,' until my parents were judging every person I dated even once against the long-term potential of Luis, and Maxima was giving me sentimental gifts on my birthday. A music box playing her favorite Elvis song, *Love Me Tender*. A book of her aubela's recipes. An actual, un-ironic subscription to *Cosmo*, telling me it was full of great life lessons. Sometimes when she visited, she dug them out from the magazine rack and left them open to articles about pleasing my man.

So, yeah, I'd been grasping at any excuse to get out of forced proximity with Luis.

Guess who was the only person in the kitchen when I stepped in? Luis. We'd shared polite chitchat since his family had arrived, but was that enough for the scheming elders? Nope.

"Mom and your mom ran to the store," he said. I was sure they'd outfitted him in the flour-covered apron before they left.

"Where's Bill?"

"Said he had to take a call."

"Subtle."

He handed me the crinkly, splattered, yellowed page I knew without reading would be the family sugar cookie recipe. He kept the laminated meringue instructions for himself.

"You can't make those and these at the same time."

He scrunched his forehead at the page. "Why not?"

As if he hadn't been right beside me during a dozen holiday cookie conversations. "Because they need a slow, cool, closed oven and these go in at three-fifty for eleven minutes. Make the chocolate kisses or the gingerbread."

I ignored his griping and gathered my ingredients. So typical, Luis taking for granted he could do whatever he wanted whenever he wanted. Some of us had changed much more than others since we were teenagers.

"Come on, Sari-berry. You can't even smile a little?"

"I told you before I don't like that nickname. Is there a reason you keep using it despite me making my preference clear?"

The 'woah woah woah' gesture he made flung mists of cocoa powder through the air. Jerk couldn't even put down his measuring spoon before acting all hurt. I gave him a look. He furrowed. I pointed to the dust trail. He shrugged and said, "Bill and the moms always do a big clean when we're done mixing anyway."

Leaving others to clean up his mess.

Not one speck of change from our teen years.

Bill came in and hugged us each into his side. Luis discovered his ability to use a sponge, because he wasn't even entertaining enough to be a competent chaos muppet. When his maybe-future-boss was around, he started behaving like an adult.

"So, how's that whole teaching thing you do, Sarita?"

I inhaled so I wouldn't bite his head off for belittling

me. "You mean my full-time job managing a group of instructors while we bring early music learning to schools whose arts budgets have been slashed by the state? It's going well, thank you for asking. Our winter concerts were last week; I'll text you the link to the video."

I was proud of my kids; of the kids in all of my program's classes. I admit, I always wanted to sleep for about four days straight by the end of each semester, but that exhaustion was in service of making some incredible, special moments as the students performed for their families and peers.

Huh. Maybe being sleep deprived had something to do with how rushed I'd been when cleaning the cottage. And my not-good decision making when I'd left the pile of broken glass so near the door.

Luis was droning on about his own job. I slipped away to go threaten my siblings that if they didn't get to the kitchen, I was going to hide the last of the peppermint bark ice cream. Cole and Margo were off paddling towards St. Joe, but Emmeline agreed to rescue me.

"You should just ignore him, you know."

Pearls of eighteen-year-old wisdom. "It's not him, it's the parents. And Bill."

"Ignore them, too. It'll blow over soon enough."

"If you really cared about helping me, you'd flirt with him yourself."

Emmeline barked a laugh. "Oh, absolutely. That'll never mean I'm stuck entertaining him every family dinner. You're safe up in Austin. Some of us have to see him more than two weeks a year, you know."

Fair point, but I was desperate. "Come on, I'll love ya like a sister."

She pointed at me. "That's another thing. Isn't there

some kind of sister code or whatever? No poaching the exes? I'm sure I've heard of that."

Despite the nearly thirteen years between the oldest and youngest Dunway children, it was a small town and I was sure some of us must have dated the same people at some point. "I think that's only for serious relationships. Not for ten minutes of making out more than a decade ago. Don't hold yourself back on my account."

"Believe me, I'm not."

I laughed, but stifled it before we got to the kitchen. Didn't want anyone thinking I enjoyed being forced to hang out with Luis. Bill kept trying to send Emmeline into other rooms on nonsense errands, while suggesting that Luis and I work together on things any semi-experienced cook could do on her own. When Bill instructed me to crack eggs for the guy, I shot a pleading look at Emmeline. She doubled over giggling.

I left my half-full tray of unbaked reindeer cookies on the counter and treated myself to a nap before I could be roped into some other mood-destroying encounter with Luis.

FIVE

SCORCH

" I don't want these." I tried to hand back the plate. It was green, and covered with red plastic wrap, just to reinforce the holiday festiveness of the bright collection of cookies within.

She'd released her own hold and stepped back, so all I accomplished was sliding her careful arrangement of sweetness into a jumble. I sighed and leaned to drop it on the low table beside me. Went back to my guitar. I'd been out on the verandah all morning, just strumming and watching the breeze play games with the palms and dunes. Until Sarita showed up, I'd almost grasped onto some peace.

Never mind how my uninjured foot was bouncing against the deck at 140 beats per minute.

"Do you like ginger? The ginger Santas are my favorite. Nice and crisp."

"I'm writing for a summer release here, Sarita. Beach, waves, sun. No Santas."

"I admit the sugar cookies could be softer. I let them brown too long, but I was under extreme pressure. And my next-to-youngest sister, that's Margo if you're keeping track, is a real icing artist, so I brought some of them anyway."

I didn't answer, but since she was already through my front door, I don't know that she noticed.

Didn't see her again for almost an hour. Otherwise known as a gingerbread Santa, something covered in powder sugar I had to wipe all down my front to keep it off my strings, and a second Santa, because, yeah, they were really tasty.

I still wasn't great on my crutches, but I was grateful for their support when I hobbled inside to a view of her ass bent over the sofa, fluffing cushions. I mean, I'd never seen anyone fluff a cushion before, but it was the only meaning I came up with for the quick, almost vicious way she chopped at the stuffing.

I cleared my throat loud enough to break through her headphones, and my view of her heart-shaped ass was replaced with a view of her heart-shaped face. Quick as a grace note, her expression went from startled to regal, like a woman who'd never seen a broom and dustpan in her life. Much less operated them, never mind the evidence of the implements against the breakfast bar behind her.

"Hey."

She cleared her own throat, and her voice emerged as cool and above my lowly concerns as when she was foisting cookies on me. Also, her gaze didn't miss the evidence of powdered sugar on my shirt. Probably just reinforced her superior tone. "Is there something you need?"

I didn't have her pride. Why would I? Me, with my everyday background, my nothing-special upbringing, my solid-B education. One thing I'm good at is music, and people used to think cause I lucked into the wave of The

Evil Stepbrothers's success, I was due some reverence. Some glorified way of moving through the world. When I knew damn good and well that I hadn't yet proven myself. Hadn't shown anyone, not even my former band mates, that I was worth a thing in my own right. And now they'd blasted that opinion across the world, so: goodbye, glory. Hello, constant calls and messages from Pam Chang.

So it was no scrape against my soul to lay out my request to her. "Got my follow-up tomorrow. I found a local foot doctor, but I don't think I'll be up to driving by then. You happen to have time to take me, or should I call a car?"

Her quick-change face revealed a hint of ... relief? "I can make that happen. What time?"

We sorted out the details, and then we were just standing there, looking at each other, not a word to spare between us. No way for me to guess if she was even a quarter as drawn to me as I was to her. I always thought her sister Jeannie was pretty, and I liked her plenty. Smart, sharp, sly. But I was never tempted to look at her the way Brendan does. As if he can only breathe in if she's breathing out. But around Sarita, I had this unsettling twinge in my gut. My heart jammed staccato riffs whenever her eyes met mine. I spent too much time groping for something to say.

"What are you listening to?"

She fumbled the remaining bud out of her ear. "English folk carols."

I snorted.

"Don't be snide. I love them. And I have to play at our Christmas party in a few days, but I do not want to rehearse with my pianist. For the past couple of months I've been teaching first to fourth year students all the basic classics, but I want to resettle the carols in my brain so I can have some fun of my own that night."

"The guy you keep dodging?"

"Who?"

I squinted like I really was trying to remember. "Name starts with an L. You keep dodging calls about him. That's the piano player?"

She nodded. "Long story. But since a bunch of it is about Christmas and I know you're trying to stay all pure and summery, I won't get into it."

She thought she was so cute. I could throw verbal darts at her, too. "You have a favorite carol?"

"*What Child is This*. The tune is *Greensleeves*, but I like to play around with it. What about you?"

"*Daddy Got Run Over by a Reindeer*."

"Grandma."

"What?"

"Not 'Daddy.' Grandma."

I shrugged. "Mom and I always sang it 'Daddy.' And also we changed the lyrics about being sad about it."

Sarita shook her head. "You're incorrigible."

I went back to the verandah without answering her. She cut off the laugh she probably didn't want me to hear, but I did. And I had an excellent auditory memory.

She kept coming over at random times. And times I asked her to. And if she was around, I kept my guitar and notebook handy, strumming and scribbling and posing like I didn't drop the phone and pick up the pencil the moment I heard the jangle of her keys.

I was maybe too focused on everything being said about me, and about Haddon and Lewis. When Sarita was around, humming and clattering in the kitchen and once actually beating the living room rug over the rail of the verandah, I deployed any number of expressions meant to show she was disturbing me, but I also got more lines down than when I was alone.

She never called me on it. I never called her on the fact that she stopped by about five times as much as was reasonable, given that I was recovering pretty well from the puncture wounds.

The foot doctor, though, sling-shot me back into my less able days, with all her prodding and digging and deciding to glue up one not-so-cooperative gash on the ball of my foot. Sarita had to prop me up on the way back to the car, since I'd gone in with just one crutch and needed more support to leave. I barely noticed her getting food in front of me that night, and didn't even try to pretend I was going to work before crashing out.

The next morning, in the middle of another doze hopped up on pain pills, I got another call from Pam. "Yeah?"

"You might want to wake up fast."

"Why?" I stretched, yawned.

"Faster than that. Someone caught you and that woman coming out of the doctor's office yesterday. Someone else recognized her as part of the family that owns the cottage. Someone else went as far as booking a night there to get the address, and their DMs are open offering up your location."

"Altruistic of them."

"Ha."

I was on the move. At least I'd wriggled my bandaged foot through the skinny leg of my jeans before falling asleep on the verandah. "Fuck."

"You okay?"

"Can't talk and walk at the same time anymore. Fuck my life."

She laughed. "Okay, I'm going. Let me know if you need help with relocating or anything."

The way she said 'anything' shivered my hackles. "Like what?"

"Mm, dunno. Press release about your summer album. Sneak peek of a song."

"I haven't announced it yet, Pam." Superstitious of me, but I didn't want to risk TES's fanbase getting snide when I wanted everyone excited.

"Yet."

I snorted. "Bye."

Crap crap fuck. I scanned the place. Hadn't driven since arriving, wasn't even sure where the keys had ended up. I'd parked, walked the beach, grabbed my stuff from the car, but used a code to get in the door. After that it was all rushing and urgent care and Sarita unpacking for me. I limped into the bedroom, started with the duffle. Empty, and I dropped it on the bed and started tossing stuff from the drawers beside it. Bathroom? Nope, just the various items needed to keep my head and body clean. I swept everything into the shaving bag and lobbed it at the bedroom. Slid open the closet and used a crutch to drag out all the laundry I'd been stashing on the floor. The fucking keys weren't in the pants I'd been wearing when I arrived. I shook the pile but nothing rattled, nothing fell out.

Where the hell were the car keys and how the fuck was I going to escape paps or fans or whoever else if I had to limp away on foot?

I shoved everything clean into the duffle and managed to hitch it over my shoulder so I could hop-walk to the main room. My satchel and guitar case and papers and equipment were a spill across the seating area, but not a key in sight. Sinking onto the armchair, I called Sarita.

"Ho ho ho."

"Very funny. Where are my car keys?"

She paused too long for comfort. "I have no idea. Can't remember seeing them around."

I didn't answer so much as groan.

"Hey, Ignatius, what's the problem? Do you need me to give you a ride somewhere?"

"No, I need to get the hell out of here."

She made one of those placating mouth noises. "Is this … some kind of artistic temperament thing?"

"It's some kind of someone doxxed the address of this cottage and now my quiet retreat is about to be overrun by even more problems thing. And I can't find my fucking car keys to get the hell out of here."

"Oh." She just maintained her unhelpful silence.

"So can you help or not?"

"Snappy much? Give me a sec."

I did not have time for her dithering. I put her on speaker and started packing up my work. She took her sweet time, but when she spoke again I latched onto her voice like a lifeline.

"Okay, I'll be there in ten, and my family's pulling out to block whatever roads they can while we get you sorted out."

By the time she pulled up, I'd done a more sensible version of packing. Still no keys, but I spotted a news van down the road. Sarita was side-by-side with a woman I didn't know, all dolled up in a bright-ass kaftan and floppy sun hat.

I'd held the door so they could slip in, and she introduced the woman as her godmother. As soon as they were clear of the windows, Maxima snapped out of her position crouched over her cane and stripped off the hat.

"You got a ball cap of some kind?" she asked.

I looked all kinds of confused at Sarita, who rolled her eyes a tad while explaining. "Max is going to set off on a beach walk the long way home, while you put on her disguise and come back with me. We'll do a proper search for your car keys after it's quieted down some."

I wasn't in the mood to be charmed by some random older woman, even when she slipped off the kaftan to reveal skinny jeans and one of Brendan's concert tees. No one would really be fooled, with her lighter skin and reddish braid, but it was something. "You want my crutch, too?"

"I'd better, I suppose. Tedious, though."

"You'll be warm enough? Want a hoodie instead of a cap?" I waved at my duffle, like she could x-ray vision through it to see my jumble of dark clothes within.

She did have a sharp enough gaze to make me wonder how much she was seeing about me. Made me want to stand up straight and tuck in my shirt.

Instead I pulled on the disguise. Sarita's compressed lips told me I very much did not want to hop to the bathroom to check out how it looked on me. I traded sunglasses with Maxima and let Sarita shoulder my guitar.

"I'll head out now and hope that vulture follows me long enough for y'all to get to the car."

"Thanks, Max." Sarita kissed her cheek. I could almost laugh, seeing her kiss this squint-from-a-distance facsimile of me. Maybe I could plant a godmotherly smooch on her as we limped to the car.

For verisimilitude. No other reason. Not to find out if the cinnamon spice scent of her would transfer to my lips. Not to test the velvet give of her skin. Certainly not to look at her later and know she'd been touched by me.

Yeah, I believed myself.

Instead of acting on my nonsense, I slung my bags over my shoulder and tapped the floor with Maxima's cane. "Okay. Let's do this."

She tugged my floppy hat forward to better shield my face, and scoped out the view from the window.

The walk to the car sucked reindeer ass. Even unlaced, the shoe I'd wedged over my bandages was too tight. I couldn't hop with the bags and too-short cane. And every time my heel touched down, pain scraped along the ragged edges of each one of my cuts.

By the time I'd flopped in the passenger seat, suffice to say I'd stopped fantasizing over kissing the woman who was the direct cause of the injury that left me fleeing my solitude while swathed in five yards of stylized fabric flamingos frolicking among fronds.

Not to mention how many calls from Pam I'd have to field if I were caught, in disguise, kissing the woman already linked online with me. Our ruse worked on the media van, which took off after my not-doppelgänger. Turned out they weren't the only ones laying in wait, though, and the car barricades the Dunway family hustled into place didn't stop the gawkers who were on foot.

Lucky gawkers, free to wander the streets and sand.

I spotted two on the short drive, and one for sure clocked Sarita's car. Probably from the photos that outed my location in the first place, but no matter how he recognized it, he made no secret of shooting a video as we passed. I slumped low in the seat, blessing Maxima's unique taste in beachwear.

Once in her garage, she had me sit tight while she texted the rest of her family they could stop blocking off the road to the cottage. She took my bags in and returned to help me from the car. I hadn't managed to get my sneaker off in the confines of her passenger seat, so she took my foot in hand, right there in the garage.

"This is getting too familiar," she said.

"You kneeling at my feet?"

"Me tending to your hurt."

"At least you stopped saying 'ouch' every time you change my bandage."

The way she winced as I hissed in a breath told me she was biting back the word. For my part, I was biting back twelve dozen curses as she removed my shoe and the pain of constriction gave way to the pain of expansion.

I wrestled myself out of her hold and out of the car and out of the ridiculous costume and stood there, feeling barren and stripped bare, at the threshold of her life. Wondering why I was awash with the fear that if I couldn't even walk into her house as my own self, on my own two feet, I'd never accomplish any one of my other goals in life.

CHAPTER

SIX

SARITA

I tried to see our house through his eyes. He'd shrugged me off, so I just led the way in, ignoring whatever shuffling and huffing was happening behind me. I wasn't going to force him to lean on me.

"So this is us. It's a full house at the moment—or will be as soon as Jeannie and Brendan get here tonight—so I'm putting you in my room. You want anything to eat or whatever?"

Lord save me from babbling. He continued to not be forthcoming while I pointed out the various areas of the house and decided with no input to park him in the big room.

Silly name for it, but we'd called it 'the big room' ever since my parents had knocked out a few smaller rooms of the house to create the expansive but not strictly logical space for everyone to gather. The hodgepodge of bedroom extensions surrounding the big room weren't much more sensibly planned, until you looked at the layout from the perspective of the specific people who made up my family. There was nothing generic about this architecture.

My own room was tucked behind the bookcases that lined the wall past the piano. DIY sound-proofing and as much distance as possible from Emmeline's room, to accommodate both my practice and her auditory processing needs.

See? Made all the sense in the world, if you knew us.

Ignatius, though, didn't seem the least curious about the house. Another check in the 'does this guy feel any vibe towards me?' *no* column. Made no difference if I flustered around him or described my siblings in detail or batted my eyelashes and told him how super-hot I found him.

Fine. It was a one-sided vibe. I was adult enough to ignore it for the week or so he might remain in our area. I delivered his guitar and satchel to him and took off to my room with the rest of his stuff. He'd agreed to spend a night or two at the house in hopes of the attention dying down at the cottage so he could return. Least I could do to make up for the locals who'd outed him was to put fresh sheets on my bed.

A run of fast and loud chords rang out across my piano's left-hand keys, and I sank onto the bed to listen as Ignatius repeated the refrain—no, not quite. He changed the key and stuck an inverted turn at the top of the second measure. And then: a jump. Almost acrobatic, the leap to a stripped down treble clef that still left next to no space for the bass line to ghost beneath it.

And he was humming. Mumble-humming, a couple of words clear, then clearer still when he started from the beginning.

I took up violin at eight. Twenty-one years of Suzuki method, school and community orchestras, college classes, session work, teaching. Of course I'd written the occasional song. Well, set a poem to music or came up with variations on another piece, but I knew musicians, songwriters, composers.

It was somehow entirely new, spying on Ignatius as he traced a path to a song.

And he was about to be interrupted. The front door and garage door both squeaked opened, and the whole house sprang to vibrant life.

I moved to intercept my family, who didn't tend to be subtle. Ignatius glanced my way, so I pointed to my bedroom. "Need a hand in there?"

He shrugged and turned back to the piano. "I'm gonna stick on this for a bit, if no one minds."

"No one minds." I set off to prove my statement was true.

By the time I'd curtailed everyone in the kitchen and thanked them for their help and checked that Maxima didn't want anyone to pick her up, I remembered why I'd been making excuses to hang out at the cottage since Scorch's arrival. Margo and Emmeline were bickering over nothing, Larissa decided she and Alfie and the baby should just stick around for the day to help set up for the party, as though grilling me about the man on the piano was necessary prep. Cole was filming us all and I didn't need to ask to know he'd have edited footage with snarky captions loaded to social media within the hour. And Uncle Bill had arms wrapped around me and Luis both, acting like we were all on board with his plan to climb on the roof and install more Christmas lights.

"Max has his crutch." I almost sounded sorry to ruin Uncle Bill's plans. "I need to help get him settled and change the bandages."

"I never knew you had this Florence Nightingale side to you," Luis said, and I remembered every time he'd taunted me after that party that divided my teen years in half. I remembered how Maxima and Bill and my parents interpreted that taunting as flirting, reinforcing their conviction that spending time with him was one reason for my shift from unmanageable middle child to responsible daughter.

Cole and I traded looks, and he put his phone away. "I'll help y'all out."

Luis's scoff was maybe only loud enough for Bill and I to hear it, but Cole was no fool. He stepped close enough to make Luis assume his puffed-pigeon upright posture. Cole just grinned. "Come on, dude. I'll hold the ladder for you."

I slipped out from Bill's hold and kissed Cole's cheek. "Thanks, dude."

He smirked—'dude' was always the word we used when we talked about Luis—and I skedaddled before Bill could invent some other way to rope me into Luis's company.

Catching Ignatius trying to balance himself and his stuff while leaning on the cane, I slipped beside him and took the guitar in one hand while wrapping the other arm around his waist. He didn't bother to acknowledge me, other than leaning into my shoulder. Which was fine. Gave me time to think about the play of muscles under my palm and the sensation of heat leaping straight from his body to mine.

Once I'd settled him onto my bed, I pulled myself together and aimed to be efficient and as close to impersonal as I could get while cradling his foot in my lap. "Any more pictures get out?"

"Nope. Not so far, at least."

His jeans were skinny. Not even sure how he threaded his taped up foot through them to start with, but thanks to his fashion choices, I was groping all up his calf to clear the fabric out of my way. Wasn't the first time I'd noticed the scar a couple inches above his ankle; was the first time I felt the dichotomy of his crisp leg hair giving way to smooth scar tissue. Impersonal, that was me. I filled him in on doings at the house. He asked me about the collection of ticket stubs on my bulletin board. Most were for chamber music events, but I got to gigs and concerts that passed through Corpus fairly often, back in the day. And if I could find a ride, we'd head as far as San Antonio for someone worth seeing live.

"I'm just not picturing you as a groupie."

I rolled my eyes. "I had my wild phase. But groupie? Nope. I'm not on this earth to throw myself at guys who think knowing a few chords makes them irresistible."

"Ouch, as your students would say."

"Ha."

"Tell me more about this wildness you claim you had."

"It was mostly normal teen stuff: parties, some sneaking alcohol and so on, refusing to do anything expected of me." Except violin. Reconcile that image: the rebel girl who still practiced an hour or more a day and clung to her first chair position with a ferocity that matched that of the dragon tattooed around my hip. Even back then, I looked enough like my oldest sister Larissa to appropriate her ID and tell the artist my fifteen year old ass was nineteen.

Who knew that, more than a decade later, I'd be eyeballing a sketch of that dragon where it sat above my childhood desk, wondering if Scorch Madigan, of all people, would ever see the inked version on my flesh.

Or if he even wanted to. Or if the wanting, the questioning and the filling my head with fantasies of his fingers tracing her pastel scales was entirely one-sided.

He definitely wasn't saying anything to clue me in. And for the life of me, nothing gracious or suggestive came to mind to help me figure him out. I smoothed down the fresh tape on his bandage and stood, gathering the detritus.

He cleared his throat. "When are you going to look for my keys?"

Okay, so he wasn't sitting there consumed by lust, it seemed. I checked the time. "I'll head over now. Is there anything else you need from the cottage?"

He looked to his bag. I wasn't going to unpack it this time. Not so good for me too remember the texture of his clothes, the way it would slide and rasp under my hands. I had tactile enough memories as it was.

"No, I'm good. Just the keys." He shifted a little closer to the headboard and reached for his bag. "Thanks, though."

Really, there wasn't anything else to say. I left him to it.

CHAPTER
SEVEN

SCORCH

She was such a prickly pear of a princess. Like, how dare I accuse her of being a groupie? It wasn't like I was picturing her waiting for me, specifically, at a stage door. Talking her way into my green room. Shining her eyes at me while she told me all the things about me she couldn't resist.

I flipped open my composition notebook and scrawled out all I'd been fleshing out at the piano. It was one of those sudden burst songs, the kind of that left me wondering if it was as good as I thought, or if I was churning out the tritest sentiment ever set to music.

Sometimes it turned out to be trite. But this time ... this time, I was confident. Almost confident. Confident enough to work it up so I could play it for Brendan later.

Good thing, since I was halfway through my beach time, and determined to meet my timeframe for the recording studio. I'd thought I'd be writing catchy, bright, indie rock about grabbing your power and using your voice to reject everything holding you back and, of course, falling in love. Cause what's an album without a healthy dose of falling in love?

And everything I'd written since stepping into that pile of broken glass was fighting me. All the love was tied up at an un-crossable distance. All the power was challenged by unrelenting doubters. Nothing basked in the sunshine; nothing lifted into a playful breeze. But this new song. It was daydreams in a hammock and waves smashing the shore. It pulled at me.

It was the sound I'd been aiming for.

I hoped it was the sound I'd been aiming for.

Could have been minutes or ages, I wasn't much paying attention, before someone knocked.

"Yo."

Brendan came in, lifted my guitar off the bed, and settled himself beside me. "Merry Christmas."

I wrapped my palm around the fret board to stop him strumming *Silent Night*. "Humbug. I'm in summer mode. How's it going?"

He filled me in on the latest, and I thanked Jeannie for bringing me a slice of Brendan's apple pie, and we all were settled in, laughing and loud, when Sarita returned. She and her sister were real sweet, leaning into each other for a long hug. Didn't realize I was humming until Brendan elbowed me and asked what the song was.

"What?" I thought back. "Not a song. Or not yet, maybe. Just tumbling around."

He made to flip through my notebook, like I'd let that happen, then grinned and started picking out my melody.

"Do that in A minor."

Brendan backed up a couple of measures and took my suggestion. I tapped my thigh a moment, then found a fresh page to compose in.

"If they looked over, they'd see my eyes rolling so hard," Jeannie said.

I ignored her, but did jerk my head up at Sarita's laugh. It was all-new to me. Not the wry simplicity of earlier conversations, or the snarky doubling-over of her haunted whooping crane story. This was big enough to fill the room, clear and colorful like faceted crystal.

It vibrated inside me.

The sisters started to leave, but I had to hold her in place, just for another half minute while the sound waves of her laugh spread to fill her room. And my gut. "Sarita."

She stilled at my quiet tone. "Ignatius."

Brendan's snort was too low and deep to disrupt the resonance of the room. I thought of something to ask. "Any luck with my keys?"

She lost the smile. And when she answered, her flat tone killed all the reverb in the air. "No, not that I could find. I can only suggest you unpack all this to double-check. If you don't turn them up, maybe the rental agency can get you a spare."

She and her sister took off to build gingerbread houses or string cranberries and popcorn or strew fresh-cut pine boughs everywhere or some such thing.

Brendan waited until they were gone before thwapping my shoulder.

"Hey!"

"What's going on with you and my sister-in-law?"

"Nothing."

"Oh, sure. Okay then."

He did not mean he was letting it go. I kept my focus on my writing.

"Scorch. You're looking at her like she labeled and

color-coded your patchbay. I'm not saying you shouldn't; Sarita is awesome. But don't act like nothing is going on."

I shrugged. "Nothing in real life. Maybe a couple or three things in my mind."

"Hey!"

"You can't get all offended when you're the one who asked. And don't tell me I'm moving fast when you and Jeannie were in bed two seconds after meeting."

He narrowed his eyes. "Wasn't two seconds."

"And you moved to Jackrabbit ten minutes after that."

"It's my hometown. Sort of."

Ha. Keeping him on the defensive was working.

"And besides, all that's one reason I'm not saying you shouldn't admire Sarita. Far as I'm concerned, y'all should make long-term plans and make sure they include plenty of time near us. Just admit you're into her, is step one."

So much for redirection. "Okay, you want to talk about it, so. Fine. You've known her for a few years now, right?"

"Um-hmm."

"Right. So." I ran out of steam and took back my guitar.

"Was that a question?"

Snide guy. "It was an opening. For you to talk about Sarita."

"Wow, be more surly, could you? It's Christmas. Time for rejoicing and all that."

"Bah."

He laughed that super-deep laugh of his, which probably would bring half the house dashing in to find out what was so funny. "What do you want me to tell you? I mean, you've met her. You know Jeannie. You get how they're so beautiful, and so smart, and so fucking cool. I mean, Sarita's not as funny as Jeannie. That woman can make anything hilarious. You've seen how she cuts Ramon down to his knees; she's sharp as hell."

I grunted. Ramon was Brendan's manager. Effective guy, but not the most subtle or gracious.

"I guess Sarita's kind of more reserved than Jeannie. More background, or something. Jeannie lights up any room like a disco ball, you know?"

"You are so sappy in love." And wrong. I mean, no shade on Jeannie, but she was a candle compared to Sarita's light.

"Yep. I lucked out the day I finally walked back into my dad's bar."

"You're no help at all. Go find your wife and some mistletoe."

"Don't need the help of some parasitic plant for Jeannie to want to kiss me." He got up despite his taunting words, looking like someone more than determined to get his hands on his Dunway sister as soon as possible.

Not that I was jealous. As soon as I left this place, I would forget everything there was to know about Sarita Dunway. Even when I was sitting in Brendan's recording studio in Jackrabbit, having dinner with him and Jeannie all the time, I'd never be looking at Jeannie thinking how Sarita's eyes were more almond, and her voice deeper, and how, instead of Jeannie's charge-forward-and-take-over approach to the world, Sarita sits back and the world comes to take her direction.

Even when she was coming to take care of me. I wasn't sure how she ruled her space so completely, with her awareness and her expectation of cooperation and her simple sympathy. But she did. Since I met her, she'd been spinning the world in any direction she wanted, without asking permission or doubting if she had the right.

If I was jealous of anything about the whole situation of my life, it was that. The lack of doubt.

Filing away my annoyance that I was composing more productively in Sarita's populated, busy house than I had been with the solitude and wide-open vistas of the cottage, I flipped to another page and kept scrawling.

At one point Sarita came in saying, "Don't mind me," and rustled through her closet for a bit. She also scooped everything from a dresser drawer into another and left the empty one half-open for me.

Half-open, half-welcome, half-warned. Halfway to any place I can be warm.

I was strumming when Sarita slipped back in. Fresh clothes, wet hair, a bundle of jeans and such in her arms. She glanced my way and I set my stuff aside. Seemed like I'd barely moved for hours. From the other side of the door, I heard chatter. "Party starts soon?"

"Yeah."

"Oh, you sound excited."

"Hah, yeah. So excited. Listen, you need anything before I get sucked into the vortex?"

"I'm good. Maxima brought my crutch."

She bustled. It was strange, seeing her move in this space of hers. I'd watched her in the cottage, at the doctor's office, on the dunes. Her self-possession and surety.

All that was gone. Shattered. Not that she was fidgeting, or spinning out. Just moving around the room like she didn't know how it worked. Hairbrush from one place, flipping through some papers on desk before going back to the dresser and scooping her hair into a twist. Then, hair in one hand, holding various necklaces to her chest until she seemed to pick one. After that, back to her desk where she'd left the hairbrush.

"Maybe some food?"

She stopped detangling and looked at me. "Sorry?"

"I can just order a pizza or something, if you tell me this address. All my food's back at the cottage. I don't mind what I eat, but until I get word from Pam things are in better shape, I don't want to, you know, answer the door for a delivery driver or anything like that. Sorry, that probably makes me a pain. It'll be easier on your family, though, if no one is doxxing this place on top of whoever's staking out the cottage."

"Right, no. Of course."

I pulled out my phone to search for food options. "So, the address?"

She dropped her braid and shook her head. "I'll bring you a plate in a bit. We've got more than enough. I mean, you can come out to the party, if you want. I'm not trying to shut you away in here."

"Thanks, but no. I know everyone's used to Brendan and used to being cool about, whatever, rock stars in their midst and all that. But Pam's trying to contain this trash-fire of speculation about The Evil Stepbrothers. Those leaked pics didn't help. Laying low is my best strategy for now, and not just so I can get these songs in shape." I riffled the pages of my notebook with my thumb. It soothed the same way tapping it across the callouses on my left hand did. Reminded me: here I was, successful, working musician, capable of writing, playing, singing. I'd worked for it and I'd gotten it. And once Pam did her bit and I did mine, I'd come through all this with a solo album. All my own work, my ideas, my execution. No concerns about what credit anyone in TES was stealing from me, no need to practically earn a degree in accounting to figure out why the royalty statements weren't lined up with what my gut suggested should be my cut.

Sarita sat beside me on the bed, and I realized I'd the one fidgeting. I cleared my throat.

"I'll bring you a plate," she repeated. This time I just nodded in reply. She looked down, following the nervous motion of my thumb. I closed my hand in a loose fist and let it drop.

I couldn't guess what else she was gearing up to say before someone knocked on her door.

CHAPTER

EIGHT

SARITA

Everything was nonsense interruptions and hard to figure undercurrents and my looming awareness of time ticking down until the command performance I was pretending was not going to happen.

"Uncle Bill's looking for you."

I shrugged at Cole. "Does he think I'm going to rush out to find him with bare feet and my hair half-done?"

"Not to mention you only lined one eye."

I covered the left side of my face, like I even knew which side I'd missed. Cole laughed.

"Shut up."

"At least I warned you. Remember when Larissa waited until y'all were on the school bus before she asked why you were wearing two different shoes?"

"Yeah, I'm so glad you're more mature at twenty-four than she was at ten, thanks."

"It's, like, one of my earliest memories, that fight. I think you had tantrums for days. Why do you think I asked for that full-length mirror on the bathroom door when I was in kindergarten?"

51

I snorted, and he grinned. We'd had one of our first talks about his gender dysphoria while standing in front of that mirror. I was glad he had memories of it that he enjoyed owning, ones that seemed to give it a place in his history that wasn't all the work of discovering how to match his outside to his true self. Even if it did mean yet another way for him to tease me in proper younger sibling fashion.

"What does Bill want, did he say?"

"What do you think? He wants to be sure you and Luis practiced your carols."

"Nope."

"Sar."

"Well, what? I don't want to do it. They've been holding this over my head for a decade now. Why does he get away with acting the young prince while I'm forever and ever the bad kid?"

He spun me around and started working my hair into a pattern. "Got pins?"

"Inside." We shuffled to my dresser. "Ignatius, this is my brother Cole. Cole, that's Brendan's friend Scorch."

"Nice to meet you."

Cole grunted something behind me. I swept up a handful of hairpins and a couple of ties and lifted them so he'd be able to reach.

"So." He jabbed my scalp, which I didn't even bother to complain about, because getting his styling help after all the times he'd fixed up our little sisters' heads for school when we were younger meant I'd get a quick look that would hold all throughout the party. Worth it. "I know it's ghosts of Christmases past and all, but do you really think you'll get out of Bill and Mom and Maxima making a big damn fuss about the music?"

"We've got a, like, legit rock star in the house. Why aren't they making him sing?"

Ignatius shifted and started to lever his bad leg off the bed.

"Two legit rock stars," Cole said, then pitched his voice to mimic Maxima, "but it would be an imposition when they're here to enjoy the holiday and not to work."

"I'm not here to enjoy anything." Ignatius slowly crutched his way towards the bathroom.

I would have shook with laughter if Cole's grip on my updo weren't so tight. Turned out there was a reason Scorch and Scrooge shared such similar spellings. "No one's asking you to perform, don't worry."

He disappeared without answering. I glanced at Cole in the mirror. "And why is it so easy for the elders to forget that I'm a professional musician, too? They've never had even half a qualm about asking me to work during the party."

"Well, that's your own fault. You shouldn't have been so all-fired cute about performing every time there were more than eight people in a room when you were first learning violin. You set the pattern; they're just staying inside it. Plus the whole thing of you still having to prove you're a nice, obedient child. Give me another two pins."

Once he'd spun me for a three-sixty check, he told me to fix my eyes and he'd stall Bill. Leaning in, he added quietly, "I see why they call him Scorch. Wow."

I shook my head. "Shut up."

"Jeannie told me you were all melty-eyed over him, and I definitely get it."

"I am no such thing. Go away. And thanks for the warning. And the fancy bun."

He returned my fist bump and skedaddled.

I was as slow and deliberate and precise as I could possibly demand of myself with the rest of getting ready. Every mussed detail from before Ignatius offered to buy himself a pizza, I set perfectly to rights.

Like there existed even a tiny possibility that I could make myself charming and elegant and helpful enough that my parents wouldn't look at me with that eternal touch of, "we are still devastated about the night you were arrested" marring their brows. And then I would, of course, perform as they requested. Because it was a small enough price to pay for them pretending they didn't always worry I was about to turn into a disaster of an adult.

No matter how many times I paid it.

One of these days, all the dimes and nickels of my redeeming acts would add up enough for them to forgive my debt. Not the financial debt; after completing my community service hours, I'd spent the rest of that school year and all summer cleaning rooms at Uncle Bill's hotel. I'd paid my parents every cent of my fine, and the costs they'd imposed for driving me anywhere while my license was suspended. But that single Class C Misdemeanor meant the rest of my childhood—and a good helping of my adulthood to date—was spent performing responsibility for them.

And dodging Luis.

He snuck up behind me the moment I entered the big room. Or maybe he didn't sneak; he might just have happened to be there. But it had been a decade since I was willing to give the guy the benefit of the doubt.

"All tuned up, Sarita?"

Not giving him points for not using the nickname, either. "Nope."

He smirked and brushed a hint of lint from the green and red striped blazer he wore over a t-shirt printed with moody reindeer. The room was full of family and friends in festive garb, but somehow Luis was the one whose clothes made my eyes twitch. "Why fight fate? You know my mom will be announcing our performance the moment the clock strikes nine."

"If she can't find me, she can't drag me forward. You can go solo this year."

He was still all smirky, so I opted out of spending more time near him. Mingle, chat, nibble, drink. The usual. Fun, yes. I was enjoying it all; Mama and Dad and Bill and Maxima knew how to create a bash, that was always true. And just being with all my siblings again—the six of us huddled behind the tree for a few minutes, catching up. So much better than only joking with each other via group text.

Maxima knew right where to find us, though. "Hey, baby, it's almost time for carols."

"Oh, Max, how about we change it up this year?"

She laughed like I didn't mean it. "Go grab your violin."

Cole chimed in. "Yeah, Sar, we're all ready to sing."

My always-helpful sisters seconded and thrided and fourthed and fifthed him. Not one of them was fazed by my glower. I stuck out my tongue, because when has being with my siblings not caused me to revert to childhood, and headed to the buffet table. I hadn't yet fed my hidden guest. And piling up tamales and queso for Ignatius gave me an extra few minutes before I had to face the one family holiday tradition I loathed.

CHAPTER

NINE

SCORCH

Three songs in a day.

Fire. All the bullshit—influx of fans, lost keys, running away in disguise—-and I'd written three songs. Of course, I was such a grumpy asshole that instead of being stoked I was back on schedule, I was mad I'd done it under all the pressure.

Same thing happened to me on flights. Get me to thirty thousand feet and lyrics poured out of me. Those bursts of creativity never bothered me. I took them as a gift.

Better not say anything like that to Sarita. She'd go on about Secret Santas or something.

She came in with dinner and a margarita, which wasn't enough to make me confess to my productivity, but did make me realize how hungry I was. I moved to her desk to eat and just about fell off the chair at my first bite.

"Better than pizza?"

She acted all innocent, like she didn't know my taste buds were partying. I tried the second flavor—spicy bean— and groaned.

"Mama always said the whole point of having so many

kids is so she could divvy up jobs at our tamalada. I was on salsa this year. Try the verde."

I wasn't about to stop her being smug about it. I'd even concede that she'd discovered a Christmas tradition I hundred-percent approved of.

Sarita pulled a violin case from under the bed.

"Why do you keep it there?"

"I don't. But when I was changing the sheets for you I tried to make more space in here so you could get around."

"Oh, I see now. You were afraid I'd knock it over with my crutches."

"That too." She tightened and rosined her bow before playing across the strings. Everything was flat.

I hummed an A for her, and she wrinkled her nose at me before adjusting her fine tuners.

"I got it."

Ha. I gave her my grumpiness along with my perfect pitch. "Yep, you're all set."

She didn't love me taking credit for her tuning, that was for sure. And, yes, it wasn't like I hadn't noticed her great pitch while she was going around my cottage singing at random hours of the day.

I devoured the rest of the pork tamale and started on the queso. "So, you've given in about performing?"

She grunted. Effective as a non-answer answer. I was over my writing grump all the sudden. If that made me even more of an ass, well. At least I wasn't mentioning it. Great to know I could always be worse. "Thanks for the dinner."

Something taut about her unstrung. She sank onto the edge of the desk beside me. Maybe it was the gold in her top or the warm glow of her exposed neck. Or just the fact that she'd let down her guard and that alerted my own it could take an unscheduled break. Whatever it was, nothing was bothering to interrupt the exchange of heat between us. When she said, "You're welcome," it sounded more like an invitation than a response. And I always did like getting exclusive, elusive invites.

So I accepted. I filled the inches between us. Took her hands in mine. Slid them onto my chest as she slipped into my lap. All those other things—the need to create my own anchor in life, everything that went down with TES, Sarita's over-the-top devotion to Christmas traditions—I jettisoned. All I had left was her heat and her eyes and her touch and her smile.

Before I could so much as stroke a tendril of her careful hairstyle, the door opened. A half-second after the knob turned, someone knocked, and a half-second after that, it turned out to be one of those guys you have to look twice at to see if he's good-looking or just highly groomed.

"Ready, Sari-berry?"

Sarita flinched and I trapped her hand between my waist and my palm. She squeezed, making me glad I kept up with the ab work even when I was busy feeling crap about whether I was going to have the career I craved in five years.

She sighed. "Yeah, two minutes. And if you keep calling me that I'm spilling eggnog all down the back of that jacket."

He didn't close the door when he left.

"So that's Maxima's son?"

"Yep."

"Cute."

Her face. The contortions she went through to stop herself, I was guessing, from giggling. I lifted her hand to my lips, because how was I supposed to send her off into some snake pit I didn't yet understand without at least one taste of her skin? And she was all spice and fire, cumin and chili and everything nice.

"Drink your margarita, you. Apparently I like you lots when you've got a bit of hard liquor in you."

"I think you like me fine even when I'm sober as hell."

"I think you want to think that." She stood, sighing. "Need anything else?"

I floated my hand down her hip and said, "Let me put it this way: I don't need you to bring anything back with you when you're done making merry."

Another laugh. It didn't expand into the room as much as I'd have loved as she left. But what sound waves I captured in my chest, I decided to hold on to as long as I liked.

Thanks to the unusual way her house was laid out, the party was happening just on the other side of Sarita's bedroom door. When I heard cutlery clinking on glassware, and the sound system cut off—thank goodness because even with the door closed it was an overload of holiday songs—I made my way to the threshold and took a look. Sarita and the guy in the loud jacket were standing by the piano. A man with Dunway eyes and a snowman sweater had arms around them both, cheerfully commanding the room.

"Allan and Carmen said I could be the one to make the welcome speech this year. I get to do it once or twice a decade, if I've been helpful enough setting up their tree and didn't eat too much of Allan's favorite fudge." He timed his pause for laughter like a true showman. "Seriously, though, as always I'm so grateful that Carmen and Allan invite me to co-host with them every year. This party is one of our family's favorite traditions, and we hope it is for y'all, too."

He went on in that vein for a bit, and never once did Sarita look over at Maxima's son. She mostly made goofy micro-expressions at couple of her sisters—well, one I knew was a sister, from seeing her pass by earlier, and the other looked like if Sarita had glasses and a pixie cut—who were standing off to the side of her. They both bit down on their lower lips and I glanced real quick to catch Sarita with the tiniest flare to her nostrils and eyes a bare fraction wider than usual.

Uncle Bill—I'd gathered that was his name—released Sarita and the other one. Luis. I was turning into an expert on the Dunway circle of acquaintance, which a day ago I'd have said was unnecessary to my ongoing life. So, Bill lifted his arms and clapped his hands once and said, "And now one of the best traditions we've got for this night. My beautiful niece Sarita and Maxima's handsome son Luis have been performing carols for us all for, what is it now? Almost twenty years, right? And every year they're more in tune with each other than the last. It's been one of the big joys of my life, I don't mind telling you, to have witnessed them learning and growing together. Together. That's what I value most about the holidays, the togetherness. And that's what I love about these two talented performers, how well they balance each other and play off of each other. And maybe I'm biased since Sarita's Allen's daughter and Luis is becoming one heck of a manager for Maxima, but don't they look great together?"

He held for applause again, and the sisters—there were three of them gathered by then—regaled Sarita with super-slow nods and golf claps. I'd go viral with the gif if I'd been filming it. She aimed a wide, clenched-teeth grin their way. Bill told everyone to raise their glasses of eggnog and toast to togetherness, then steered Luis to the piano seat while everyone clinked and cheered.

So now I knew what snake pit she'd been avoiding. Bill made a point of being obvious about pushing the two of them together, but I hadn't seen either Sarita's or Luis's parents stepping up to tone him down. Maxima—now in a chic silver and blue kaftan that I could barely believe shared suitcase space with her flamingo one—stepped forward before they could start playing to take an absurd number of photos of the two of them with instruments and the Christmas tree in the background.

Once at the piano, Luis nodded at Sarita, apparently not at all bugged by parental machinations, and started the intro to *Hark the Herald*. When Sarita's violin came in, I found myself leaning forward in the doorframe, snagged by her skill.

He ... was competent. He kept time just fine, his dynamics were good, he came in with a serviceable tenor that encouraged the other guests to sing along. But she was the star. I knew she'd been playing forever, studied and made a career of it, but knowing paled compared to hearing. To watching her command of her instrument. And I didn't mean that in a dirty way, no matter what other ideas I had about how she could work with her hands.

When Luis tried out a flourish that had no place in the final stanza, Sarita cut him a look he ignored. Then he changed the tempo with no warning while she was playing a descending run. I didn't know what the deal was, but my best guess had to do with him not liking looking less competent than her, so he tried to throw her off. She wasn't having it, which jibed with the Sarita I was coming to know. She kept the tune under control, and as everyone was applauding afterwards she and Luis went into a whispered conference. He shook his head. She shook hers. He shook his again, and she nodded. The crowd watched and occasionally called out suggestions.

She tossed her head in a manner that suggested she was clearing her hair off her shoulder, though her brother's many hairpins had yet to budge, and tucked her instrument under her chin. One short nod, and she'd launched into *Joy to the World*, while Luis pretended not to glower. At the end of the intro, his fingers jumped to pound out the opening to *Jingle Bell Rock*. The sisters kept singing *Joy* for a few measures, but most everyone else shifted to the less musically complex option.

I'd heard more than enough. By the time all necessary rocking 'round the Christmas tree had ended, I'd strapped on my guitar and excused my way to the front of the crowd. A couple of camera phones were aimed at me, enough to make me glad I hadn't splashed salsa on my shirt. Luis didn't notice me until I found a wall to lean on, dropped my crutch, and lifted my chin at Sarita. She stepped closer, which was all the permission I needed to play an opening for *What Child is This*. Sarita caught what I'd thrown her, and wasn't shy about trills or frills as we bounced off each other. All throughout, her smile was generous, but it was the lift of her brows and the glint of her eyes that sucked me in.

When we finished, I asked, "Next?" She compressed her lips and I started to laugh at the first notes of *Carol of the Bells*. Even Christmas-loving people like those at this party weren't up to the task of singing along. At least, not until Brendan pushed his way to stand beside us and carried the "ding dong ding dong" on his own. In his famously deep voice, it was somewhere between hilarious and captivating. Jeannie passed her phone to her brother so he could film while her shoulders shook, so I guessed she was in the hilarious camp.

Brendan side-hugged Sarita as our final notes hung in the air, whispering in her ear before nudging Luis off the piano bench. He introduced himself, as if that was necessary, and told everyone to gather round for a medley of carols. Sarita handed me my crutch and took my other hand once I'd rested my guitar on my back.

She was tugging me towards her room, but I'd already flung myself fully into Christmas mode. May as well get all I could out of it. "Come here first."

"Where?"

I nodded upward. "Just there."

She followed my gesture and raised her eyebrows. "Oh, really?"

"Yep."

"Remind me to bring the tequila and limes to your cottage once the coast is clear. I like this side of you."

"Give me some time, I'll be sure you like every one of my sides."

She laughed, but it was a quiet one, just for me. Her family and friends were singing *Silent Night* right behind us, and it was a trick to navigate violin, guitar, and crutch, and not a bit of all that put a damper on the party that was just the two of us when we kissed under a sprig of mistletoe.

TEN

My siblings, once in a good while, could band together to be total sweethearts to one of us in need. Sometimes it was arguing Jeannie's case when she bucked Dad's dream that she would take over the business. Sometimes it was taking shifts to stay with Larissa and the baby when Alfie was offshore. And sometimes, it was creating a human wall to stop anyone taking pics of Scorch Madigan making out with me in the middle of the big room.

They gave me almost a minute to press tight against him and wrap my free arm around his back. To open my mouth to the captivating warmth of his. To feel the rumble of his humming chest against mine.

And then someone—turned out to be Cole—took my violin from me and jabbed my shoulder to get us moving. The human wall moved with us, a truly nonsense endeavor, what with Ignatius half-hopping while leaning on me. I kept giggling. I kept wondering what I was up to.

We made it to my room and by the time I'd helped

Ignatius to the bed and handed over his guitar case, half the Dunways were in with us.

"Right. Out. Go." None of them budged at my demand.

"Tell Brendan thanks," Ignatius told Jeannie.

"Oh, I'm thanking you instead. I haven't enjoyed any Christmas party half as much as this since I stopped believing in Santa."

Before they could devolve into the story of the time Emmeline figured out the Santa myth before Margo and ruined her big sister's entire December, I herded them to the door.

And locked it.

Awkward. "Too awkward?"

He laughed a little. "A little. But worth it. To me, anyway."

I covered my cheeks with my palms, but they would not obey my order to cool down. So I packed up my violin, because that was something I could draw out for ages if I tried. Wiping down the strings. Double-checking the rosin was in the storage compartment. Aligning the velcro strap over the neck so it was lined up just so. But I didn't want him wondering while I worked, so I said, "To me, too."

"You know, I'm an injured man. I can't get all performative about my feelings, stride across the room and wrap you in my arms, any of that. You're going to have to come to me, Sarita."

How did those words make me blush deeper but bounce with pleasure at the same time? I liked the feeling of power he handed over so readily, that was one thing. All his experience being the big, famous guy, and he didn't have an outsized ego. Not in this.

And if he could be honest and eager and kind all at once, I could get over my blushes.

So I went to him.

He lounged back on my bed, which he'd cleared of all his stuff. Funny, seeing his notebook and pen side-by-side with my e-reader and hand lotion on the bedside table. For all the times I'd felt a bit like we were playing house at the cottage, it wasn't a place either of us fully inhabited. But he'd slotted right into my space, in this childhood bedroom where I'd planned out a life free of domestic details.

"So, you just couldn't resist my English folk songs in the end?" I kicked off my shoes and hitched a knee onto the bed.

Ignatius grinned that brimstone grin of his. "Don't think a couple of carols and a snowman cookie mean my heart's grown three sizes or anything."

"No?" Settling beside him, I traced a heart on his chest. "Seems to be a pretty big organ to me."

Clever man, capable of swiveling us so he pressed me to the bed, all while guffawing. "You want to see an organ grow three sizes, Sarita, I've got you covered."

I had to bite my lip before asking, "So you're a grower, not a shower?"

He growled into my neck, and I shivered from clavicle to clit. The shivers didn't last long, though. As he kissed his way up my jugular, they became pulses. Throbs. A moan that rose from my core and wasn't dampened at all when our mouths, finally, met again.

Oh *damn* was this a hot kiss. I pulled him closer, and, honestly, the thrill of touching with both hands. For both of us. The mistletoe moment had been electric and exciting and enticing.

But twice the hands, none of the audience, and all our agreement that this was actually happening? It was an infinity of chemistry.

All his dark hair and dark eyes and dark intent focused on me. It dissolved every scrap of aggravation about the ways my family saw me, about the ways they thought to fix me. It set in stone my already-solid lust for him. It made us feel like equals.

Things were moving both fast and slow. Devouring, intent, constant kissing and touching. But languid at the same time. He'd parked his body on top of mine. We weren't rolling or writhing or ripping off our clothes. I arched my back some. He rotated his pelvis an inch or two. Our shoulders rubbed together. I hooked a foot over his calf, but even in my horny haze I remembered to be careful of his injury.

Know what a man with famously strong vocals has? Excellent control of his lips. And tongue. And timing. It was make-out heaven. And his body language was full of sin.

"Sarita."

"Mmm?"

"Fuck me."

If only it had been a request. But, no. He rolled off me and we both sank to the mattress, groaning. Our locked door hadn't done a thing to truly isolate us from the raucous party. I didn't know who was knocking, but they were doing it loud enough to be heard over Mariah Carey's *All I Want for Christmas is You* floating from the sound system.

"Do you think I can get away with pretending to not hear them?"

He snorted.

"You're no help." My grumbling didn't stop him from sidling over to give me a brief, sweet, promising, closed-mouth kiss. It may have prompted his gentle push to my upper arm, though.

"Yeah?" I opened the door to my dad. "Oh. I mean, hi. What's up?"

His gaze hopped from me to my bed and back. Every second he stood there was erasing a year from my emotional age. "The Baldwins are getting ready to leave and want to say goodbye."

I touched the back of my head. And ignored Ignatius's suppressed laugh. "Okay. Great. One minute."

Dad was all about reminding his children we could still get embarrassed around him, and didn't leave right away. He turned toward the bed. "I'm Allan Dunway."

Ignatius had sat up and tugged his clothes in place, at least. "Scorch Madigan. Thanks for taking me in today."

"Good to meet you. And it's no problem. Help yourself to some dessert, too, if you like."

Without a clue to show if he meant that for real or as a sarcastic jab, Dad nodded at us and left.

"Come here."

It was gentler this time, his command. Still sexy, of course, cause what about him was not sexy? I pushed off the doorway and sat beside him.

"Let me fix your hair a bit. I don't have your brother's skills, but I can get you from sex hair to social hair well enough."

"Social hair?"

"Stop laughing. Hold still."

I tried, and a glance in the mirror before I went to be a nice host showed I would pass muster. Cole and Margo still gave me side-eye, but they were gonna do that regardless. See if I let them come to my place to do laundry once they were back on campus.

As expected, it was over an hour before I got back to my room. Brought a plate of dessert and a half-full blender of margaritas with me, cause I'm generous like that. While I washed out my hair and changed to yoga pants and a tee, Ignatius made a nest for us on the bed.

Safe to say neither of us was feeling shy anymore.

We shared a serving of tres leches while I leaned against his chest. No fair, really, since I was left to hold the plate and my fork while he only had his own fork, leaving a hand free to trace the muscles of my thighs and the curve of my belly.

Finally, I balanced our dishes on the nightstand and twisted to face him. "We gonna talk?"

"Like a midnight confessional?"

"Yes, tell me all your impure thoughts." My solemn tone was a little undercut by the way I was tracing his pecs and abs.

"I will if you will."

God, all the things I could confess if he got me started. But that wasn't quite what was on the agenda. Yet. So I settled my heart and took his face in my hands. "Ignatius."

"Sarita."

"Are we just fooling around here? Or is there ... hmm."

"Is there what?" He cupped my hips and smiled. Not the wicked devil smile, not this time. Something so much softer and more open. All this time spent observing him, pretending to avoid him, teasing him. And then this. This emotion, this connection. This sudden opening to a more personal side of him.

I fought to not lurch at him. Who knew what giddiness and hope my expression was revealing. "Is there forward momentum here? Between us? When Jeannie and Brendan get nosy—and I'm surprised they haven't knocked the door down already—are we telling them to not make a big deal out of us being thrown together just for the holiday? Am I going way overboard when all you want, still, is to be left alone? To find your keys and get as far away from this intrusive town as possible? Maybe I'm convenient for now but not … not in a way that leaves us open for more?"

Each time he flexed his fingertips on my ass, I got braver about naming my questions.

Oh, fuck. He bit his lower lip. I stopped being capable of speech.

Slowly his mouth spread into a grin, and he stared deep and unwavering at me. And he said, "I don't think I have ever met anyone less convenient than you, Sarita Dunway."

CHAPTER

ELEVEN

SCORCH

I couldn't track the nonsense pouring out of my mouth, but it was easy enough to stop. All I had to do was exactly what the hell I wanted to do: kiss her.

Did I have answers for her questions? Not as such. What I did have was the awareness that my attraction to Sarita had been growing since the moment I saw her. Every time she let loose her irritation while helping me with my foot. Each of her attempts to foist Christmas joy in my face. Her hair that went everywhere and the Cupid's bow in her lip and the way she sighed after reading her texts. I wanted to plant myself in the first carriage for the roller coaster ride of her emotions.

I disentangled long enough to tell Siri to add the roller coaster line to my notebook. Sarita poked my side. "Are you writing songs or are we smooching?"

"Can't I do both?"

She shook her still-damp hair back and gave me one of those regal looks of hers." Well, if I'm not holding your interest, I can go help clean the kitchen."

"Don't you dare." I pulled her on top of me so we'd both be perfectly clear just how interested I was.

"Oh, you did grow three sizes after all!"

"Hilarious." I thrust my hips at her. "So. About this house. Do you have issues with having sex here while your whole family is watching *It's a Wonderful Life* in the next room?"

Her hands tickled up my ribs as she drew up my shirt. "Please. We don't watch that until Christmas Eve. If they watch anything, it'll be Charlie Brown."

"So that's a no?" I sat up to get the shirt off, and raised my brows to ask if I could remove hers, too. She did it for me.

No idea what I'd been saying. Brain wasn't that functional anymore. "Is that a dragon?"

She very helpfully stood to remove her leggings and give me a full view of the ink wrapped around her waist.

And of the rest of her, which was also captivating. *Damn.* "Damn."

She mimed a curtsy, which might have been elegant if I wasn't only watching the way her breasts swayed as she moved. I glanced at the door to confirm it was locked, pulled back the sheets, and finished stripping.

"Damn your own self." She shimmied out of her undies and I groaned. And laughed when she leapt onto the bed beside me. "So, I know you just had a tetanus shot and lots of antibiotics. How's your sexual health?"

So blunt. And a bit bossy.

I liked when we were bossy with each other. It felt like give-and-take and collaboration and respect. "Clean, as of a couple months ago, haven't been with anyone in three."

Sarita did the math, seemed to come up with an answer about the tour with TES, and licked her lips instead of answering. "Okay. Great. Me, too, except I was seeing someone until just before Halloween, but we always used condoms."

"You okay with that?"

"What?"

I tapped her heart as I tucked us in to be nude in our cocoon of blankets. "Feelings stuff?"

She laughed. "Oh. Yeah. It was casual, and he met someone he wanted to be exclusive with. Friendly parting."

Turned out I did know some kind of answer to all her questions about us, because the idea of a friendly parting was like a pebble in my shoe. Or a shard of glass in my foot.

"I've got condoms in my bag."

"I know. I unpacked them last week."

Kissing impertinence was as fun as kissing lust and kissing triumph and kissing camaraderie, with Sarita. She pointed at the overloaded bedside table and I took her direction. But no way was I going to roll on the condom I found there until I'd explored more of her body.

She had a hell of a good body. I traced curves and rounds, hollows and nooks. I threw out every expectation I'd built up after the other times we'd touched. All her care-taking, bandaging, lending me a shoulder. None of that had clued me in to the way we would combust off each other. And she was firing, too. Touching, too. Tracing, too. My nerve endings sparked every place her palms stroked. And plenty of places they didn't.

Couldn't have that. Time to re-calibrate all that give-and-take of ours.

I edged below the blankets. Now this was something I enjoyed far more than the Christmas cookies. Sarita tasted warm and wicked, slick and sweet. And she bucked into my mouth, taking and taking and taking all I gave.

And I gave. I gave until she broke.

She laughed when she came. That big laugh, the one that thrummed throughout my chest. Belly shaking, hands curled on my scalp, one heel firmly planted at the top of my ass. I swear even her clit quivered with the laugh. Kissing my way back up her body, I murmured questions about noise, about happiness, about consent. She rolled the condom on me as soon as I'd planted a knee beside her beautiful hip.

Her breath had no rhythm. Her cheeks glowed. "Ignatius." She used my real name, and everything about me stuttered and surged straight at her.

Clumsy as I felt, urgent and tangled in sheets, in limbs, in emotions, we were both grinning. We kissed, we whispered, we rolled and rocked and flexed and flowed.

"Wait."

I froze. Well, I was molten, so I tried to freeze.

Sarita inhaled deep, her chest expanding and distracting me. But her eyes re-captured me fast enough.

"Waiting."

She pulled all her hair up and behind her, a twist that fell immediately but maybe pulled her words tumbling out as well. "I don't require answers to all my questions from earlier."

The aloof way she tried to speak while perched in glorious nakedness above me made my balls tense up, ready to sprint headlong for our orgasms. I ran the calloused tips of my left-hand fingers along the ridge of her dragon's back, then danced them at the top of her folds. She rose, just a tad, just enough that I could spread her wider and see the base of my cock rising into her.

"I don't mind what questions you ask, Sarita. I'll answer them all."

She didn't move, so I did. I rested my thumb lightly on her clit, and because I'm a rock star with well-honed timing, I used my other hand to give her ass a slap. Just forceful enough to propel her forward into the circles I was drawing with my thumb. She sank down to take my cock to the hilt. I levered up to take a dark, tight nipple into my mouth as she rode me, her pace and the fingernails she drove into my shoulders all the encouragement I needed to hold back. To revel in the way her muscles gripped my achingly hard length. To graze at her neck. To yank her close for a kiss that muted our moans as she clenched me tight. As, together, we came.

CHAPTER

TWELVE

SARITA

After we kicked off the covers and collapsed side-by-side. After we caught our breath and I passed Ignatius a couple of tissues to wrap up the condom. After I muffled a giggle in the outstretched bulk of his bicep.

After another kiss.

That's when we talked some. I don't know why I needed it, the talking. After a decade of being sexually active, after partners casual and serious and everything in between, why, with this man, was I so intent on definitions and clarifications right out of the gate? Because he was friends with Brendan and my sister? Because my face was already circulating online in connection with him? Because of the niggling feeling that his fame put me on the wrong foot somehow, when it came to the power balance between us?

Because something about being with him felt different —more intense, more important, more inexplicable—this time?

I did not know. Or I wasn't brave enough to face any answer I might know.

Whichever; we talked.

"You're good in bed."

How was he suddenly able to make me laugh so much? I bit that firm muscle on his arm again. "You're okay your own self."

He wrapped his too-tortured limb around me and pulled me close. "Thanks, I'm flattered."

I snorted and he tickled my shoulder, which set me back to giggling. "Okay, we've established we weren't inventing the chemistry. How about ... you know, everything else?"

Damn, but his chest was a cozy place to rest. Bonus: we were staring at the dim ceiling above instead of at each other. For all the recent intimacy, I was feeling more stripped bare by the talking than I'd been by all that actual nudity I'd chased us into earlier.

All that actual nudity had been a brilliant move on my part. My body was still humming and jumping. I absolutely planned for us to fuck again, and soon.

Now if my brain would stop humming and jumping so I could tease out what I wanted said.

"I may not remember all you asked, before my synapses exploded. Something about telling Brendan?"

Deep breath, comforting heartbeat under my ear, everything outside my door muffled and distant. "I guess, yeah. It's not that I think anyone's unclear, after that kiss out there. Or that I mind them being all gossipy about it. Fill the halls with speculation; we're adults. Plus you accomplished your mission."

His chest rose fast below me. "What mission was that?"

"The one where you pull me away from Luis and stake a super-public claim on me."

He rolled and hovered above me. Kissed me like, *wow, yeah*; a definite claim of a kiss. Got that demon grin back on his smug face. "I did, didn't I?"

"Yep. And thanks. Whatever I have to deal with from the elders will be worth it, now that I can get through the rest of this holiday without having him shoved at me every three seconds."

"Will it be bad?"

"The interrogation?" I shrugged. "If it is, it's overdue. So it's fine. I mean, I might need a few more orgasms to really balance the scales, but I'm guessing we can work on that."

He wasn't hard—yet—but he thrust at me with intent anyway. "We can."

"Superb."

He distracted me from the next thing I wanted to say. When we eventually got back to talking, he told me he was open to making a relationship with me fit into his life. "I already plan to spend a lot of time in Jackrabbit recording at Brendan's studio in the New Year. It's just a hop from Austin, right?"

"Everyone always with the bunny jokes." I moved so we were curled face-to-face. It didn't unsettle me anymore, seeing his expression while he explained his thoughts. Damn this proof that I was drawn to him in fascinating but frightening ways.

"And you? Ready to put up with my whole weird lifestyle and maybe having to tell your boss your name will be linked to mine?"

I gulped. He was regarding me so seriously, so tenderly. Like it mattered to him, that I would take a few things as given so we could go forward to find out what else a relationship would take out of us.

Probably I was blushing. Probably the lamplight was

enough to make that clear. Probably the way my heart was thrumming screamed my response loudly enough for whoever was still clattering away in the kitchen to be clued in.

But I'd set us on this blunt path, so I didn't leave my answer up to body language. "I'm ready."

We celebrated our accord in ways that conked us out for the night. In the morning, after my oldest sister sent a series of a dozen texts until I woke enough to answer her, I cleaned up and helped Ignatius settle into the big tub with a cup of coffee and a couple of pastries. In total contradiction to the stuff I'd done to help him out at the cottage, doing so didn't feel in the least domestic. Maybe he seemed more like a guest at our family house. Maybe after all the ways he'd tended to my pleasure overnight, our dynamic had shifted. Taking care of him was turnabout instead of penance for how I'd endangered him in the first place.

Not as equitable: the panel of elders facing me across the dining table when I grabbed my breakfast. Mama and Dad and Uncle Bill all settled in and watched me eat my egg and chorizo taco. Disconcerting, that.

"So." Mama: mincing words but conveying everything with her tone.

"I wasn't expecting any kind of jack-in-the-box surprise arrival in the middle of the music," Uncle Bill said. He was good at filling anyone's silence. "I could have introduced Scorch if you'd just told me he was going to interfere anyway."

"He wouldn't have interrupted if Luis wasn't deliberately screwing up the songs."

"Oh, it's his fault you didn't bother to rehearse with him like I asked you to?"

"Uncle Bill, we didn't need to rehearse. I taught him

every one of those piano parts years and years ago. My second-year students had that music memorized by Halloween. I'm not saying the sing-along isn't great fun for the party. But whatever he told you, Luis was ignoring my cues on purpose."

"Sarita."

I glanced at Mama and sighed. "But I'm sorry the carols didn't go as expected."

"I wish," Dad said, "that all of this drama with Scorch and Luis wasn't bringing out your ... you know. All the behaviors. I just want you to be settled, Sarita."

I sipped my tea and half-smiled at Cole and Jeannie, who came in and sat either side of me. There wasn't much else I could do, except give in to the confrontation I'd warned Ignatius about.

Cole jumped in. "She's had the same job since graduation, Dad. And she makes dinner for me and Margo like twice a month. I don't know how much she needs to do to count as settled for you."

"And I hope I'm proof that being with a musician, or being a musician herself, isn't some sort of problem," Jeannie added, toying with the platinum band on her ring finger.

"You kids always gang up when you want me to be wrong."

I refrained from rolling my eyes, though I couldn't have been more tired of his argument. "It's not ganging up, Dad. It's presenting evidence so you can evaluate your unconsidered statements and be gracious enough to admit you're wrong."

Mama sat forward; Jeannie set a palm on my forearm; Uncle Bill pointed at the ceiling; but it was Dad who won the race to respond first. "You want evidence, Sarita? Sneaking out, partying, drinking? Getting arrested?"

"And when did you stop all that? When you were dating Luis." Bill's pointer finger indicated the door. As if summoned, my nemesis and my godmother entered. "So put that in your evidence pipe and smoke it."

Could the room be more crowded? I had three more sisters, two brothers-in-law, a nephew, and the guy I'd been kissing under the same roof. Maybe we could rig up a speaker system so no one missed a second. Whatever air my family hadn't squished out of the room didn't feel like it was getting into my system. Dad and his brother with identical 'proved our point' pursed lips. Maxima eyeing me like she'd never understand anyone who didn't rush into her son's arms. Luis standing there all smirk and silence.

I wasn't having that.

"You think it was one date with Luis, of all people, that stopped me? I mean, first of all, y'all have always been pretty quick to demonize my teenage behavior. Okay, I partied. I drank, I snuck out. I made out. I admit all that. Even though I wasn't doing a thing that Luis and so many others were."

He, of course, snorted at that and put his arm across Maxima's shoulder. "I wasn't all that bad, was I, Ma?"

"No, you know what? You kinda were, but also? Whatever you were or weren't doing, doesn't matter. Because whatever I was or wasn't doing that shocked y'all, know what else I always did? I maintained my grades, I made All-State Orchestra, I cooked family dinner once a week. Before my arrest and after, I was always responsible like that. Settled into the mold y'all wanted like that."

Mama half-raised her brows, but my tirade was fueled by Luis's sneer.

"And the main thing? The main thing that night was, I was looking out for my sibling. Okay, not the way y'all might've wanted, and I'm not talking about his taking the risk of going out as his true self that night. That work was all Cole's. I'm talking about being the good sister you always asked us to be. Looking out for him when he was in a new situation, making sure he stayed safe when things went to shit. Excuse my language. Getting him a ride home, even when it meant I was arrested, because I headed back into the party to find Luis. Who was my date that night. Who had taken off without a word to either of us. Who's never bothered to mention, not in almost a dozen years, that he was the one who took us to the party in the first place. On a night we thought we were just going to hang out with a few kids from his school, he drove us two towns over and then bailed when the first siren blared."

Uncle Bill spluttered, which wasn't something I knew I could identify before I saw it happen in front of me. Mama turned her stare on Luis, who smoothed his expression into the one he thought passed for innocent.

"That 'date' the week after the party? Yeah. That was the third or fourth time we'd gone out. And I wasn't going to tell you about that time, either. I only went to see if he had anything to say about bailing on Cole and me that night, which, for the record, he did not. But he managed to imply things about us once I was towing all your lines, to give himself some sort of credit for my penance, and not one of you ever questioned it. Instead you've spent a decade or more trying to push me at him, and it's enough. I'm done covering for him, and I'm more than done letting y'all tell me I'm messing up every decision I've ever made."

CHAPTER

THIRTEEN

SCORCH

"Y̶ou took your thirteen-year-old sibling to a high school party?"

I'd been lurking behind my kaftan-donned friend Max long enough to hear Sarita's speechifying. And now her dad was jumping straight over every one of her points to land on a criticism.

"Luis is the one who took us," Cole said. "Sar is the one who got me out."

"Have you also been buying booze for Margo during all those Austin dinners you made her?"

Okay. No. Polite as I could be, I tapped Maxima to let me through. But Sarita was on it. "Margo has been twenty-one for almost a year now, and no. But yeah, I let Cole come with us to the party, and I got drunk at the party, and I got arrested. There were other parties, too. Before that. I drank at them, but I never got caught. And maybe it wasn't Luis's fault that he took off without us, maybe if I'd been as good at self-preservation, I wouldn't have worried if he was there or not and piled into my friend's car with Cole. Maybe if I hadn't been as drunk, I'd have just called him to see if he was out safe and concentrated on keeping myself out of trouble. Instead, I did it the way I did, and I ended up with a juvenile record and community service and that job cleaning for the hotel. Which, for the record, thank you, Uncle Bill, for giving me the chance to earn what I needed to pay back Mama and Dad."

"And thanks for never telling on us when I took her shifts so she could go out with her friends."

Mama looked at Cole. "Excuse me?"

He shrugged. "Only here and there, that summer. I always felt like I should help out, since it was my fault she got caught."

"It was not." Sarita bumped his shoulder with hers. "But I totally never minded handing over the rubber gloves and trolley to you."

I laughed. Talk about insight into how much Sarita resented every bit of the cleaning she'd done at the cottage. A nice topping to all the insight about why she'd been so intent on doing it despite her gritted teeth.

Of course, the laugh got all those people at the dining table to register my presence. Luis was slinking into the kitchen behind me, and Maxima wasn't trying to stop him. I stood clear, one crutch and one foot grounded on the floor while my body yearned toward Sarita. "Hey, babe. Looks like it's gonna rain. You up for running me back to the cottage so we can check outside for the keys before every-thing's all damp?"

Jeannie hid a guffaw in her shoulder, but I was sure she'd be reenacting this whole scene for Brendan later. Cole's dimples popped when he bit his lips to keep his laugh almost sub-vocal.

She, though. Sarita. A shoulder like her sister's, hitched coyly. Dimples like her brother's, bloomed in full on her cheeks. A body I felt yearning in reply to mine. As she stood, Maxima huffed and followed her son out of the room.

"Ten minutes. I'm need to reload the dishwasher and shove a few things into a bag."

"I'll do the kitchen," Cole said, a wry undercurrent to each syllable.

"No one ever does my chores for me," Jeannie pouted. Her father shook his head at all three of them.

Sarita stopped when she was close enough to take my free hand. "Mama?"

Carmen flicked a wave at us. "Go."

"I don't think I've been so hard on you kids, have I? If you didn't want to perform with Luis you could have just told me any time." Bill wasn't as on board with this being over as his brother and sister-in-law, it seemed. Or else, they weren't on board, but they were employing a strategic retreat.

Well, good for them, if so. That was my plan, too. Sarita kissed them all and led me out through the kitchen, where we did spend a few minutes organizing the breakfast detritus in a way that would be easier for Cole to process.

A not-so-brief stop under the mistletoe, and we ended up back on her bed, cuddled but chaste. Sarita wrapped herself big-spoon style around me and shook her head between my shoulder blades. "Your timing is impeccable."

"I aim to please."

"You heard the whole story of my reprobate teen years?"

"I told you before, I adore all the tales of you being a bad-ass rebel."

She mashed her forehead more tightly to my spine and I felt unstitched by the pressure. Like my ribs could expand more, my nerves could sense more. The alchemy of my body with hers. I tapped a syncopation to capture the thought. She repeated the rhythm on my chest and I realized my hand was on her arm. We copy-tapped a few more beats at each other before the ping of drops on her window disrupted us.

Sarita rolled away and stood. "So much for beating the rain."

I flopped to my back. "Is it going to stop our escape?"

"Not hardly. I'm spending the night at the cottage, yeah?"

I jerked my chin up to agree. While she packed, I did a visual sweep for anything I might have left laying around. Pam had coordinated with the local deputies to keep an eye on the cottage and move lurkers along, and done all that was reasonable to suppress the parts of the internet that were trying to fuck with my life. Well, with my physical location. Not much any of us could do about the memes or the quizzes or the general rumor mill, though I wasn't going to stop brooding about all that.

Sarita roped Brendan and Jeannie into helping with my stuff and driving us to the cottage. They stuck around long enough for lunch and teasing and some of that sibling decompression where the sisters rehashed some of the party events, elevating the drama of the high points and taking the sting out of the boorish parts.

Right as they left, the storm started. We stood on the verandah, pressed into each other's sides, watching the lightning move across the ocean-wide sky. As the pelting rain increased, the palms and sea oats became blurred shapes waving in the distance. I felt Sarita shiver and rubbed my hand down her arm. "Well, so much for combing the beach for my keys."

She waggled her eyebrows and backed through the

doorway. "Darn. Looks like we're trapped here together."

"Another unintended consequence of us coming here with toothbrushes and a bag of leftovers and sending our transportation away."

"Who could have predicted it?" By the time she'd backed to the bedroom door, she'd shucked her jeans and was holding out a strip of condoms. I abandoned the crutch and flung myself at the bed. Talk about motivation to recover from a puncture wound—if I put up with just a touch of pain, I could move fast by hobble-hopping on the heel of my right foot. And getting to the bed fast meant getting my clothes off fast and getting Sarita's bare skin on mine.

It was dark before we got around to foraging for more food. Still rainy, which I liked as an excuse to stay in, besides the side-benefit of keeping people from bothering to hunt me down. It wasn't just sex that kept us under the covers so long. I had something like a hundred questions about her life, after the party and the various currents and undercurrents I'd caught at her family home. Okay, she'd already told me some of it, back when she was forcing cookies and carols on me. When I was being a grumpy Grinch. But the context of all those Dunway relatives under one twinkle-light-strung roof sharpened the stories.

In return, over the next couple of days, she interrogated me. Not about the band, not about all the nonsense rumors, not about any of the things that ended up in articles. She'd Googled me, of course, but it didn't seem like that explained her line of questioning.

Hell if I knew how to handle the concept of someone new caring that much about me as a person. Ridiculous big-headed bullshit. This is what happens to young jerks who stumble into fame before they've ever left their hometowns. Or perhaps that was just me. Either way, I hadn't made new friends that weren't also somehow wrapped up in my career since the freshman bonding activities at UNM. Sarita discovered the silly story behind my pumpkin tattoo. She asked who my godparents were. And she dragged out my weird relationship with my dad and how that turned me into such a humbug about Christmas.

It wasn't that we agreed about everything—she kept being wrong about road trips and the joys of pineapple on pizza—but fuck it was fun to hang with her. We'd already talked about seeing each other after I left the cottage, but one morning I woke up and she was laying there being gorgeous and warm and peaceful and inspiring and so sexy beside me. And I wanted so much to decree that I was done, that she was the one for me, that nothing more needed to be said.

I bit my tongue, because falling this fast for someone rocked my world but wasn't something it seemed wise to blurt out before coffee. All day, the idea was there, tumbling around while we loafed around the cottage. While she curled on the chair reading as I engraved two of my songs. And after I eased my foot into my loosest shoe and we took a limping post-lunch walk among the dunes. The whooping cranes were digging up food from the still-damp sand, and let us wander close enough to see them clearly before they got territorial at us.

It felt like a good sign. That night—Christmas Eve— Sarita found my car keys in the sofa cushions. I tucked them in my music bag and told her she was my good luck charm.

"Ha. I think it's the miracle of the season."

"Nope. It's you. You've been good luck for my music, too. I left Arizona with my head a complete fucking mess. Those asses Lewis and Haddon tried to convince me I couldn't write unless I had them to collaborate with. And now, my songs, especially since we went to your house? It's flowing like a dream. Wait till I play them for you. You'll see. The longer we've been hanging out, the more I know I haven't fucked up everything by leaving TES. Imagine what I'll write once we're hanging out in Jackrabbit. I can't wait to get recording."

Her eyes were wide. It made me realize I'd been expecting some sort of dreamy, enthusiastic agreement.

"That's ... I'm excited for you, Ignatius."

Wow. If that was her excited voice, I'd been miscalculating how much she'd enjoyed the past few days of fucking. "Not sure I believe that, babe."

She wedged herself on the seat beside me. I snugged her hip to mine and breathed easier at the contact. "I don't mean to be weird about it. Sorry. Of course I'm glad your album is shaping up, and from what I've overheard, it's going to be excellent."

"Where's the 'but'?"

She ran her nails down my scalp and cupped the back of my neck. "No, I'm serious. It's only that it's odd to think of myself as a ... a component, somehow, of your work. I don't want to be an object to you, even if that object is objectively good. You know?"

So much for my easier breath. So much for all those times I'd reveled in Sarita's challenging nature. So much for my nascent optimism about the new album.

I nodded, and her hand dropped away. "Sure. That makes sense. Didn't mean to make you feel awkward. Or used."

"It's not—I mean, I definitely understand how feeling, you know, good emotions in general could be great for your work. That's why you came out here to start with, right?

Soak up the sea and sand and get in the summer mood, so it'd come out in the songs? I think it's amazing that you can do that—take all these endorphins we're generating and use it in your songs."

So now I was at the mercy of chemical reactions. Way to prove Lewis and Haddon's point, since the whole of my writing on our last album was me channeling my frustration about the direction of our group. I'd tried to engineer my own summer-in-December vibe but until I was sparking off Sarita, the songs weren't there.

I came to the cottage to prove to myself I have what it takes to be a solo success. And I found out not only that I need the emotions of some kind of relationship to work, but that the person who'd most inspired me, utterly rejected that role in my life.

I nodded again, because what else was there to say? She'd dealt the blow, and it wasn't like she didn't understand what I'd been trying to tell her. She got it. She just opted against taking it.

Sarita pressed her lips together. "So, Cole's swinging by in a few to pick me up for church. You still don't want to go with?"

My smile felt bitter, but I kissed her before she stood up. "No, let's stick with the plan."

"I can have him drop me back after, if you want me to spend the night after all?"

"And have your dad launch into a speech about Christmas morning and family traditions and everything he expects of you? Better not. We can make up for it later."

She held my hand a moment before slipping towards the bedroom to get ready. I sat alone in the gathering dark, wondering how to reassemble all the shattered shards of my confidence.

FOURTEEN

SARITA

Would it be such a bad thing, if Ignatius Madigan thought of me like a kind of safety net? If it was just, like, a touch of security while he launched his solo career? It didn't mean I'd turn into some kind of talisman for the rest our lives.

I tried to not argue with myself during the Christmas Eve service, because that wasn't even close to the way I wanted to honor the season. But huddling in my super-cold-and-empty bed that night, aching for someone—Ignatius—to curl against, to fill both my mind and my body, I couldn't escape my thoughts.

How much was my fear about how intense everything felt between us? How fast and unlikely and fun and unexpected it was? I wanted to discount fear. I always wanted to discount fear, in whatever I did. But if I'd mastered that, I wouldn't have spent over a decade trying to convince my parents that they didn't have to worry so much about me. Not that I'd even been successful, hence their constant pushing of Luis and local jobs and savings plans and regular dental appointments.

Seemed mostly like I needed to convince myself. To just be myself, and trust that they would adapt. They'd learn I could adult with the rest of them, or they'd worry regardless of how many times I mentioned my retirement account.

I sat up, grabbed for my phone. Texted Cole: Do you think I turn myself into a kind of puppet of The Good Kid around Mama and Dad?

Cole: And a very Merry Christmas to you, too

Me: *eyeroll emoji*

He knocked before entering my room. "I could have been asleep."

"You? When you have at least two hours of footage to edit?"

If we'd still been texting, he'd have replied with his favorite 'whatever' gif. "Fine. I need a break anyway. Why do you think you're a puppet?"

I passed him a pillow so he could lean more comfortably against my footboard. "I just wondered if I've been all show with them. Trying to convince them not to always think the worst will happen to me."

"I just figured it was your middle child way of getting attention, like the partying used to be."

Huh. *Ow.* I dug my knuckles into my sternum. "That's what you figured?"

"Hey. Everyone knows I'm the one who won the 'pay attention to the middle child' game. You can't compete, but it's cute of you to try."

"Goddamn it."

"You can present me with my trophy any time now."

"Hold your breath, bro."

He pretended to, and I kicked at him. Of course, my legs were still under the covers, and his weren't, so it wasn't the kind of sibling bickering that would cause Santa to leave coal in my stocking.

"Okay, fine, I'm desperate for attention from my parents. Or siblings. Or someone. Big surprise that being one of six kids makes people a little attuned to that sort of thing."

"Call me emotionally brilliant, but I'm guessing all your angst has something to do with the singer-songwriter you left on the beach?"

"Isn't your break over?"

"Nice try. And here I've been workshopping new Insta bios. 'Five sisters, but only two of them sleeping with rock stars' is the front-runner."

"Cute." I steeled myself and confessed. "I'm freaking out about how much I like him."

Cole pretended to collapse with shock.

"Shut up. Isn't it weird, though? I've barely known him a week, and he's talking about all the ways we can see each other once we leave here."

He wasn't even trying to play sympathetic. "How terrifying for you. All the adoration. All the intimacy. All the sticking up for you. No wonder you're sleeping here tonight."

"That's so no one has to deal with a parent fit tomorrow."

Cole scrunched his brows at the screen of his phone. "'A kind of puppet,' this says. Interesting."

"Fuck off."

"Way to stay on the 'Nice' list."

I shrugged. "Past midnight. Sleigh's been and gone, nothing Santa can do about it now."

"Except make a note for next year. Anyhow, speaking of

lists, what's the pro/con situation with Scorch? I mean, con: dating a guy called Scorch, but besides that?"

"I call him Ignatius."

"Mmm. Much better."

So much sarcasm so late at night. "It's his name, Cole. And he likes that I use it."

Cole snorted a laugh. "Right: good sex in the pro column."

"Yeah." I grinned. "And he's not a morning person, and he loves Tex-Mex, and he and Brendan are friends which is probably a good signal about his character."

"Brendan is still friends with Ramon." Ramon was our brother-in-law's manager and was not known for an excess of civility.

"Okay, a mostly good signal about his character."

"I'm not sure if you're doing pros first, or if you just don't have any cons to offer up. Except that whole thing about you being scared of your emotions."

Yeah. That whole thing. One more advantage of staying under my covers for this chat: I could curl up and pull the blanket over my head and pretend my brother didn't notice me moaning into my pillow.

His kick wasn't hampered by the bed linens, so his aim was more precise than mine had been. I pushed myself to sitting and glared. "Fine. The fear is the biggest con. But seriously, Cole—what if I'm making a big mistake?"

He shrugged. "What if you are?"

"Well. I mean. That would suck."

"Sure would."

"You're not supposed to just agree like that."

"Oh, because I'm not the best example you know of someone who had to accept the idea of 'what if' while facing his fears?"

Damn him and his valid points.

"Look, Sar, here's the way I see it. You leap into this relationship, accepting that you both are at least starting out hung up on each other, and it works or it doesn't. Or it works for a while. Whichever it is, you'll get an answer you can trust, because you'll have put the time into figuring it out. The other option is to chalk it up to a holiday fling and move on, but never get those answers. And maybe Mom and Dad would like that better, for their whole 'ensure Sarita is never in trouble again' agenda, but that's not the puppet show you're tuning in for anymore."

"You are such a brat."

He lifted his camera to start recording me. "Here we are: not yet dawn on Christmas Day. Everything's all potential. The gifts are still wrapped. The brunch casseroles haven't been baked. No one knows who will end up with this year's wonkiest knit scarf from Maxima, and no one knows who'll get the last slice of pecan pie."

"Dibs."

"No calling dibs until we've all had our first slices. So let's zoom in on Sarita Dunway, slumped on her bed, at a crossroads. Okay, sitting up straight in her bed, at a crossroads. And with crossed eyes—stop that. If you make me laugh it messes up my Serious Narrator Voice."

"Can't have that."

"Nope. Now tell us, Sarita, my chronologically closest of sisters, future star of my thesis film—okay, it's a featured part, but you'll be named in the credits—what does that brave beating heart of yours tell you about this impulsive but intense new relationship of yours?" He kept the viewfinder steady at me, kept silent while filming who knew what expressions crossed my face. I'd be grateful for the low lamplight, but Cole wasn't a film major for nothing.

He could turn any kind of sub-optimal smart phone footage into something cinematic.

And hell if his bravery in putting his art out there, his voice and his truth, didn't strike me as worth emulating in whatever small ways I could manage. Telling the elders what really happened at that party had made me feel strong and like I was inhabiting more of myself.

How much more of that would I get from working with Ignatius towards a way for us to be together, while still being the best of ourselves?

"And ... cut."

I blinked. Focused on Cole. "I didn't give you an answer yet."

He hopped up and kissed my forehead on his way out the door. "You sure did, sis. Merry Christmas."

After a moment sitting with the silence, I turned off the lamp and nestled down into a sleep of sweet, hopeful dreams.

CHAPTER

FIFTEEN

SCORCH

I paced, pretending it was to test the weight on my foot.

I packed.

I bundled the sheets and swept the floor and re-stacked the books on the shelves and checked the bathroom drawers.

I paced some more, and yes, the foot hurt, but I'd be able to drive. I made up a first aid pack to keep in the front seat with me, stashed everything else in the trunk, checked the time.

It was Christmas morning, and it seemed like even the whooping cranes were busy with family time. Sarita had asked me to show up for their whole big breakfast and gift fest, but she was the only one I had a present for. The only one I wanted to see.

The one I didn't know if I'd see after today.

After she'd left for church, I'd been stuck with only myself to talk to. Stuck with her words playing on repeat through my mind. I mustered up every argument I could: selfish proclamations, beseeching justifications, jerk-face demands. Eventually I had to take her statements at their face value. Accept them instead of arguing against them. Process what they might mean for her, and what they did mean for me.

And then I wrote a song. And slept. And woke to a cool, clear morning with the icy clear knowledge that I needed to leave.

Cue the pacing and packing and puttering until I couldn't delay any more. I saluted the cranes and backed away from the cottage. Sarita's house was packed with noise and activity and holiday baking smells and festive detritus. Half the people were wearing silly hats or were draped with ribbon and gift tags.

Not Sarita. Sure, her polar bear vest coordinated with the snowflake vest on one of her sisters, but once she led me to her bedroom I could almost forget about the holiday.

"I missed you last night."

That was a balm. Words to tuck in my heart next to the ones about seeing her as a person instead of an object. "I missed you, too. How we're things with the family?"

"There's no shortage of baked French toast if you haven't satisfied your sweet tooth in a while."

At that, I had to kiss the sweetness of her mouth. That heart face tilted to mine, and she tasted like mint and coffee, and smelled as always of her own unique, compelling spice. Yeah, I was a goner and a half over this woman. "So."

Her hands were on my ass, which I didn't mind even a little. "So." She rocked her pelvis at mine.

"I wish we had the privacy for that."

"You can't be quiet?" Damn, but she had the best suggestive, naughty expressions.

"Funny, I think that's your entire family three feet on the other side of this door. Can that baby open doors yet?"

"He can barely crawl."

"So it's only the other dozen people who might walk in on us."

She laughed. "I was going to argue your numbers but I'm a little worried to realize you got it right. Come sit. Tell me what you got up to last night. Did you finish the roller coaster song?"

I traced a finger over her knuckles. "Sarita."

Her hand flexed in mine, then went still. "Ignatius?"

"I'm sorry I objectified you."

She was shaking her head before I finished speaking.

I went on, because waiting wasn't going to make it any less wrenching to say. "I know there's more to it; I think you know there's more to it. But, babe, I'm so into you."

"Why does that sound like a bad thing? Ignatius, I'm sorry, too. I—"

"No, let me finish. I mean, I'm sorry for interrupting, but I need to say this."

Sarita laced our fingers together and turned her body towards mine. She didn't look certain, but she did nod for me to continue.

"Okay. Thanks. So into you. And it's overwhelming, and I'm pretty much the definition of in flux at the moment, and I need to be sure I'm being careful with that. With me, and with you, with our emotions. Because I think what I want—what I'm positive I want—is to go deep with you. Fairy tales, happy ever after, the stuff songs are made of. And maybe you want that to, or can come to want that. And maybe we can go from me on crutches a dozen days ago to the two of us walking securely together into the future, and it would be nothing but solid ground."

Damn but she was pretty. I soaked up all the emotions playing across her face. She opened her mouth, raised her brow at me. I smiled. She took a deep breath. "Okay. Yes."

"Yes?"

"To the going deep part. Just, if you're in the midst of all this evaluating and deciding, you should know, I'm there, too. Sounds a lot like we both had similar thoughts last night. For whatever that's worth about this whole rest of our lives thing."

I yanked her in for a kiss. Everything in me was a volcano and I was moving tectonic plates of expectations to re-form the landscape to suit us.

She nipped at my lip and I traced her teeth with my tongue, lost to everything but the pulse of my heart, and hers. We broke apart, but not far apart. Sarita straddled me, hands stroking up my arms. My palms were planted on her hips. Our gazes were locked on each other.

"I'm heading out."

She blinked. Tilted her head and blinked again. "You're ... what?"

"That's what I figured out. I can't afford for you to be right. We can't afford it. I have to head to Jackrabbit now. To be by myself for a while, like my original plan."

"Because of the solid ground thing?" She sounded so sardonic.

Was this doomsday? Just when I thought we'd been wrestling our way to the same conclusions? I tucked her hair behind her ear. "Yeah, because of that."

She leaned forward, pressing our torsos together, and it was tender instead of erotic. Our breaths rose and fell together. "I don't want you to."

"I don't want to, either."

She nodded, her head shushing against my shoulder. "And that's why you're going."

The relief of knowing that she understood, that she agreed. The pain of knowing that she wouldn't fight to change my mind. I kissed her head. Her neck. Her clavicle, even though I had to nudge aside the silly Christmas vest to reach it.

"For the record, I'm staying in Texas for ... well, for however long. Not just to use Brendan's studio."

"No road trips?"

"Ha. Not unless I can convince you to come with me."

She faked looking at a watch. "When are those pigs scheduled to fly again?"

"Well. Seems like we're doomed from the outset."

The way she smothered me in kisses suggested she didn't agree.

Never mind the people on the other side of the locked door. We moved to the bed. Because that volcano of mine was eager to help create the best solid ground for us. As soon as I got her out of the holiday vest.

CHAPTER

SIXTEEN

SARITA

Walking Ignatius to his car, past the gauntlet of parents and siblings and Uncle Bill's partner who'd shown up while we were in my room, did not fill me with warmth and joy.

Every reason he was going matched every reason I needed him to go. To embrace his talent without reference to me or anyone. To slam the brakes on our headlong rush towards commitment and ensure we wanted an enduring relationship outside the snow globe of the holiday. To give his PR person the chance to build as much of a privacy wall around us as was reasonable. To give me time for an honest talk with my family when we weren't besieged by Christmas to-do lists.

We kept up a friendly facade until we'd gotten outside. Somehow, seeing his rental car at the curb of my family home, waiting to whisk him away, popped the bubble of bliss we'd been floating in so often since our first kiss. At least, that's what it did for me. His expression suggested something similar.

I did a quick check for anyone spying at us. Only my

baby nephew pulling himself up on the windowsill inside. "So."

"So."

"Your foot's okay for driving? You've got my address, all that?" I smoothed my hand over my fluttering heart while he pulled out his phone to check.

My own buzzed in my pocket. I smiled at him. "Sexting already?"

"Funny. It's your Christmas present."

"And here I thought you going down on me was my present."

"Funny even more. That's something you can have anytime. This is a special occasion gift."

No reason to cry. Not really. Three days, maybe four, and I'd be back in Austin. Plus, all those reasons.

Such logical reasons.

Fuck.

"I know I'm a grouch so you may not have noticed, but it's been incredible to get to know you, Sarita. I'm not saying we might not screw it up, but hell if I'm not looking forward to keeping you in my life."

My goddamn heart. And tear ducts. And hands, lips, lungs. Nothing about me wanted to process the moment. I was melting and burning and Scorch Madigan, my Ignatius, had slipped past my defenses.

"Not a chance of getting rid of me now," I said. Fingers crossed it was a Christmas wish that would come true.

"Call me tonight?"

I nodded. Kissed his again. "Text me from the road. Not while driving. Be safe. Stop if the foot acts up."

"I've read the aftercare instructions, too, you know."

I sighed. "I know. You've got me all twisted and fretful. I don't even like nursing people."

"Ouch." He said it just the way I always did, taking the sting out on himself for me.

"Ouch your own self. Okay, you should go now or I'll drag you inside and tie you to my bed."

He laughed. "Promises, promises."

Another kiss, and there was nothing left to say. I swiped under my lashes while he got in the car and dug the heels of his hands into his own eyes. My lips held the ghost-pressure of his. My cheek tingled where he'd stroked it. My soul stretched after Ignatius as he drove away, and the best I could manage was the sit on the sidewalk and watch his car round the corner, away from me.

Eventually the concrete seeped hard and cold through my jeans, and I slouched back inside. No one stopped me from going straight to my rumpled room, from sinking onto the bed that smelled like Scorch and sex, from laying in a half-daze while I committed everything about the previous dozen days to memory.

When at last I pulled out my phone, I found he'd texted me a sound file. *Winter Sea Song.*

He'd written me a song. Taken the *romanesca* from *What Child is This*, twisted it away from *Stairway to Heaven*, and flung it across our sand dunes. It took four replays before I could get through it without crying. But those damn tears were gonna fall no matter what I did, so what better impetus than my own gorgeous, melancholic song?

Eventually I took myself off for a restorative shower, then slipped into the kitchen to help myself to some of the spiced cider warming in the crockpot. Larissa and Margo were in the dining room, and gradually the rest of us gathered there, too. Sibling telepathy of some sort.

"You okay, Sar?"

I rested my head on Jeannie's shoulder a moment.

"Yeah. Just trying to figure how to break it to Cole and Margo I'll be spending my weekends at your place for the foreseeable, so they have to find someplace else to do their laundry."

"You make me play therapist in the middle of the night and this is the thanks I get?" Cole asked. Margo flicked his forearm, but they were both laughing. I relaxed a fraction more, each moment we sat there. Even when Margo pulled the UNO deck out of her cardigan and we got cut-throat with each other. It was their way of offering comfort without making me rehash everything I was feeling. I smiled across at Cole. Turned out the middle children did get attention, when we really needed it. Just not always in obvious ways.

Later, I played *Winter Sea Song* for Brendan and he helped me figure out the remix I wanted to do. "Send me all that, and the original, and I'll get it done when I get home."

The remaining days at the house crawled by. Uncle Bill cleared out, along with Larissa and her family. I readied the cottage for the next renters, and volunteered to do the deep-clean of Mama and Dad's kitchen. The baseboards still bore evidence of the mess Luis made with the cookie mixes. Not to mention masa in the predictably unpredictable locations. Under the microwave. On the side of the stove vent. Along the edge of the sink counter.

"Thanks, Princess. You always do the best job in here," Mama said.

I took off the rubber gloves to recapture my hair in my scrunchie. "Sure." Because I could operate on her terse level when I wanted to. And calling me 'Princess' was downright effusive, for Mama.

"You'll see your musician soon?"

I nodded. My stuff was ready to go as soon as we finished breakfast the next day.

"I'm happy for you."

With that, Mama went away. So I guess she, at least, was learning to adjust her view of me. I sent the verbatim conversation to the sibling group chat, just to giggle over Cole's and Emmeline's jealous reaction gifs.

Eventually the molasses of time released me, and I lead-footed it back to Austin. I'd gotten a bunch of class prep done in the days after Ignatius left, but I was determined to have everything organized so when I headed out to Jackrabbit, I'd be free to focus only on him. Maybe that was setting us up to mimic the vacation days together instead of whatever real life was supposed to look like for us, but I gave myself a pass. After all, it had been four full days since the man had brought me to orgasm.

Well, since he'd done it in person.

He was staying in the small apartment over Brendan's recording studio. Did I bother to greet my sister and brother-in-law? Did I stop by to wish Brendan's dad a Happy New Year? Did I get my bag out of my trunk before darting up the stairs to his door?

No, no, and not even. Clever guy that he was, Ignatius was fresh from the shower, and his place was warm, and the sweater dress I'd put up with driving in just so I'd have a half-second to lounge seductively in his doorway did a fine job of being easy to get out of.

"Hi. Underwear off. Boots on." He was tongue-deep in my belly button before he fumbled a condom off the table by the entrance.

"Hi, yourself." I sank to my knees beside him and whipped the towel off his waist. He was hard, and smelled of bergamot or some such thing, and he took off my bra one-handed while I smoothed the protection down his girth. Next thing I knew I was bent over the table and Ignatius went from shoving my panties down around my knees to licking at my cunt from behind. He kept just barely brushing my clit with his tongue, no matter how I arched my back and spread wide for access. I groaned and he responded by squeezing my thighs, which didn't do a thing to ease the wild desperation I felt. Finally he pushed two of those well-calloused fingers of his deep inside my vulva while cupping his other hand over my breast.

"I'm so horny for you. Will you please just fuck me already?"

"All you had to do was ask, babe."

Ignatius withdrew his hand and lifted my hips just a bit higher, lining up, teasing me with the head of his cock until I reached for him myself. It was just the ticket to get him to shove into me and plant a thumb right over my aching clit. I almost came on the spot. So keyed up from our absence, from anticipating this moment, from knowing we'd have forty hours to fuck as often as we could.

His mouth was on my shoulder, my neck. I was braced and bucking back against his thrusts, but I needed to taste him. Any part of him. I got my teeth into the gorgeous flesh of his forearm and groaned with pleasure. His thumb worked faster, gentler. Then slower, harder. I growled and he went back to fast and light. His cock stayed deep, ground into me, barely withdrawing before arcing back in, and then we both were chanting nonsense and sweating and cursing and clenching and coming.

Hot fucking damn.

Ignatius eased me up and stroked over my torso with the still-damp towel. We half-staggered to the sofa and collapsed, the aftershocks still sending shivers across my limbs.

"Hi."

I laughed. He kissed my temple.

"Hi, yourself."

"You just said you love me."

I thought it through. Seemed he was right. I arched my brows. "Throes of passion?"

He wriggled his own brows. "In sex, veritas?"

I laughed again. "You were a classics major, I gather."

"Amo, amas, amat."

"Amamus," I added.

"Wait, what?"

"You said 'amo, amas, amat.'"

I couldn't see the blush on his dark cheeks, but it made me giggle that his chest went pink. He winced some and admitted, "I know that's something in Latin to do with love. From a Smooth Billies song? But I don't know what it actually means."

Okay, it was official. Maybe premature by some lights, but official. I loved Ignatius Madigan. "It's one of the first things a Latin student learns. The declension of 'to love.' 'I love, you love, he or she or it loves.' And 'amamus' is the next part of the declension. 'We love.'"

"Amamus."

I nodded.

"So you admit you love me."

I nudged him. "Are you admitting you love me, or is this just some song to you?"

The man was such a good kisser. So was I. Made for a good match. "I admit everything. Amamus."

I sat with that tenderness for a moment. Finally breathed a fully-settling sigh. "Cool."

We tossed on some clothes and got drinks and I said, "I've got a New Year's Eve present for you."

"Is that a traditional gift moment I don't know about?"

"Well, not really. But you're special, so you get it anyway. Besides, I never gave you anything for Christmas."

"Cause I'm a Grinch."

"Cause you're a Grinch." I handed him my phone with the file ready to play. It was *Winter Sea Song*, but with a few bars of me singing harmony, and a violin track mixed in.

His face. His gorgeous, awed face. I wanted to take a picture so those happy eyes could stay with me always, but of course my phone was busy making music at him. "It's rough, but Brendan has the tracks so he can remix it with your originals. If you want. I...."

I shouldn't have been embarrassed. Yeah, he was a pro, and I was altering his work without even asking first, and he had every right to be offended. Plus the whole thing about not needing collaborators.

I took a calming breath. I was a pro, too, after all. "It's a signal. Or code, maybe. To tell you I won't censor you if you want to think of me as a good luck charm."

His hand was solid in mine. "I don't need you to be my charm."

Right. "I know."

He squeezed. "It's been on my mind all this time, Sarita. You were right, what you said. That I don't need you. You inspire me. You energize me. And I sure as hell want you around. I love you. But need? No. Not to do my work. It's all want, and love, and fun. And I'm the happiest ever that you are all want and fun and love with me in return."

Could a body survive this much melting and melding? I was looking forward to finding out. "Thanks. Same."

"Happy New Year, Sarita. I love what you did with the song."

"Well, I love the song. And I love you."

We weren't paying enough attention to notice when the clock struck midnight, but we definitely rang in the New Year in the best, most intimate and tender and thrilling way. And we would do it again, and again, and again, for all our years to come.

Acknowledgments

Thank you as always to my gorgeous family, especially Robert, who, honestly? Puts up with a bunch from me. Good thing we're in love.

Thanks also to Martha, for her whooping crane knowledge, and to her and Aisling and Kathy for keeping me on my feet!

My lifeboat romance group keeps trying to derail me from writing with constant chatter about all the excellent romance books they're reading, but they also helped me pick Scorch as the funniest guy version of Cinderella's name. Y'all are a great community.

Robert, David, and Kieran, your musical knowledge is such help to me. I hope I didn't mess anything up too badly.

Kieran, thanks also for getting too-well-versed in foot injury. I am still in full-body cringe mode from every article I read about foot puncture wounds (one might think I'd avoid writing about a subject that freaks me out so viscerally, but one would be wiser than me.) So it's above and beyond for my son to injure his foot while thousands of miles from home. I didn't have to look at the wound (phew!), but I had someone a text away to ask all my fun questions about crutches and infections and bandages. (He's fine. And French health care is pretty great, too!)

I love you all!

About the Author

Melanie Greene lives in a tiny woodland cottage in a big skyscraper city, with her husband and kids and pets and plants and all the people inhabiting her imagination.

For more info, visit her at www.melaniegreene.com, where you can sign up for her newsletter to access new releases and bonus content.

facebook.com/MelGreeneBooks

twitter.com/Daki_MelGreene

instagram.com/melaniegreeneauthor

www.ingramcontent.com/pod-product-compliance
Lightning Source LLC
Chambersburg PA
CBHW070504170726
48291CB00008B/2646